Tess finally got a clear view of the opposite side of the yard...and what a view it was.

Caleb had just come around the corner of the shed. He'd taken off his T-shirt, and she couldn't drag her gaze away.

He took the seat beside her. As she glanced over, she saw a long, thin scar traveling up his rib cage.

Reaching out with a shaking hand, she traced the scar. "Oh! Caleb, I'm sor—"

He lifted his hand and touched one finger to her lips. "Don't say it. I don't want that."

She sighed. "I wish I knew what you *did* want." She looked away. "You say you're here to buy property, but you don't seem interested in anything I've shown you. And then yesterday, in the truck...you said you'd gotten carried away. You said it wouldn't happen again, but..."

He leaned closer. "It won't happen again," he said, his voice low, "unless you want it to."

Dear Reader,

One of the things that will make me put a book on my keeper shelf is falling in love with the characters—the family and friends and folks from the community—who support the hero and heroine. I try to add that strong sense of community to my stories, too.

In writing my previous book (*A Rancher's Pride*), I fell hard for Flagman's Folly, New Mexico. Many readers tell me they did, also.

In *The Rodeo Man's Daughter*, an injury has put Caleb Cantrell's future at risk. Caleb has never felt the love of Flagman's Folly. Yet, knowing he can't go forward until he has settled scores from his past, he returns to his hometown. You've heard the expression "It takes a village to raise a child"? Well, in this case, almost everyone in town bands together to try to save Caleb—from himself.

I hope you enjoy this story! And please look for a third book set in Flagman's Folly, coming to you later this year.

I would love to hear from you. You can reach me at: P.O. Box 504, Gilbert, AZ 85299 or through my website, www.barbarawhitedaille.com. I'm also on Facebook at www.facebook.com/barbarawhitedaille and Twitter, www.twitter.com/BarbaraWDaille

All my best to you!

Barbara White Daille

The Rodeo Man's Daughter

BARBARA WHITE DAILLE

TORONTO NEW YORK LONDON
AMSTERDAM PARIS SYDNEY HAMBURG
STOCKHOLM ATHENS TOKYO MILAN MADRID
PRAGUE WARSAW BUDAPEST AUCKLAND

Recycling programs
for this product may
not exist in your area.

ISBN-13: 978-0-373-75395-6

THE RODEO MAN'S DAUGHTER

Copyright © 2012 by Barbara White-Rayczek

www.Harlequin.com

Printed in U.S.A.

ABOUT THE AUTHOR

Barbara White Daille lives with her husband in the sunny Southwest, where they don't mind the lizards in their front yard but could do without the scorpions in the bathroom.

A writer from the age of nine and a novelist since eighth grade, Barbara is now an award-winning author with a number of novels to her credit.

When she was very young, Barbara learned from her mom about the storytelling magic in books—and she's been hooked ever since. She hopes you will enjoy reading her books and will find your own magic in them!

She'd also love to have you drop by and visit with her at her website, www.barbarawhitedaille.com.

Books by Barbara White Daille

HARLEQUIN AMERICAN ROMANCE

1131—THE SHERIFF'S SON
1140—COURT ME, COWBOY
1328—FAMILY MATTERS
1353—A RANCHER'S PRIDE

To my readers who love the town of
Flagman's Folly, New Mexico
I hope you enjoy this chance to visit there again!
and
as always, to Rich

Chapter One

A long memory made for bad company when a man had too much time on his hands. Especially when those hands held a sizable number of grudges.

Caleb Cantrell eased up on the gas pedal of the pickup truck he'd rented earlier that morning at the airport. He cut the engine and stepped down from the cab, his worn boots hitting the ground and raising a cloud of dust. First time in ten years he'd set foot in Flagman's Folly, New Mexico, and the layer of dirt that now marked him made it seem as if he'd never left.

Yet he'd come a hell of a long way since then.

Here on the outskirts of town, he stood and stared across the unpaved road at the place he'd once had to call home. After he'd left there, he'd slept in no-tell motels, lived out of tour buses and trucks and, eventually, spent time in luxury hotels. Didn't matter where you went, you could always tell the folks who took pride in ownership from the ones who didn't give a damn.

Even here, you could spot the evidence. Not a ritzy neighborhood, not a small community, just a collection of ramshackle houses and tar-paper shacks. A few had shiny windows and spindly flowers in terra-cotta pots. Some had no windowpanes at all. Here and there, he noted a metal-sided prefab home with too many coats of paint on it and weeds poking through the cinder blocks holding it up.

And somewhere, beyond all that, he knew he'd find a handful of sun-bleached trailers, their only decoration the cheap curtains hanging inside. The fabric blocked the view into the units through the rusty holes eaten into their sides.

Sometimes, the curtains blocked sights no kid should see, of mamas doing things no mama should do.

Swallowing hard, he retreated a pace, as if he'd felt the pull of one rust-corroded hulk in particular. It wouldn't still be there. It couldn't. But he had no intention of going over there to make sure.

Across the way, a gang of kids hung out near a sagging wire fence and a pile of cast-off truck tires. Still quiet, but soon their laughter and loud conversations would start, followed by the shouts from inside the houses. Some of the houses, anyway.

The rough edges of his ignition key bit into his palm.

In all the years he'd been gone from this town and with all the miles he'd logged, he should have shoved away everything that bothered him about this place.

He hadn't forgotten a single one of them.

The gang of kids had moved out of sight behind one of the shacks. A lone boy, eight or nine years old, stayed behind and stood watching him. Dark hair, a dirty face. Torn T-shirt and skinned knees. Could have been Caleb, twenty years ago.

The kid made his way across the road. "Hey," he said, "whatcha doing?"

"Just looking around."

"What's wrong with your leg?"

The boy must have noticed his awkward gait, the stiffness that always hit him after he sat in one position for a while. "I hurt my knee. Getting off a bull."

"Thought you were supposed to stay *on* 'em."

He shrugged. "That one had other ideas." Not too bad—in those three quick sentences, he'd managed to bypass two years' worth of rehab and pain.

The kid looked away and then quickly back again, shuffled his feet and jerked his chin up high. Caleb recognized the mix of pride and false bravado.

"Hey, mister...got a dollar?"

"Sure." How many times had he asked that question himself? How many times had he sworn he'd never ask it again? He reached into his pocket for his wallet, thumbed it open and plucked out a bill without looking at it. "Here you go."

"Wow. Gee, thanks. Thanks a lot."

Caleb grinned. The boy's grubby fingers clutched a hundred-dollar bill. He turned and raced across the road as if fearing Caleb would change his mind. He wouldn't. He had plenty of money now.

Folks in town would sure be surprised to see him again, especially when he started spending that cash. When he started showing them just how far he'd come. Maybe then they'd look at him differently than they had years ago.

His grin fading, he shoved the wallet into his pocket and nodded.

Yeah. He'd show them, all right.

Too early to tackle his first order of business.

Caleb looked down the length of Signal Street, taking in the storefronts along the way. Insurance agency. Harley's General Store. Pharmacy. Ice-cream parlor and clothing store. Everything the same as he remembered it from ten years ago. Except for the real estate office he planned to visit as soon as they opened.

How would Tess handle seeing him walk in the door?

The question stunned him, making him realize he wasn't sure how he'd react to their meeting, either. They hadn't parted on the best of terms.

He turned his back on the office and found himself staring at the Double S Café. Not much to look at, just a small square structure made of stucco. But Dori and Manny had brightened the place with pots filled with cactus plants all along the front and painted flowers and vines scrolling around the doorway. Above the door, a sign showed one letter *S* hooked on to another one. The Double S. That was new since his time.

Slowly, he made his way inside and along the jagged path between scattered tables to the rear of the café. He'd spent a lot of time in this cramped but cozy room, way back when, though not as one of the customers. How could he, when most days he went off to school without even any lunch money?

He settled on one of the stools that gave him a view through the open doorway into the kitchen. The owners, Dori and Manny, stood in conversation near the oversize oven. Dori spotted him first, her expression telling him she'd recognized him right away.

They hurried out to the counter.

Manny shook his hand and slapped him on the shoulder.

He stiffened when Dori leaned close to give him a long, sturdy hug. "It's so good to see you, Caleb."

Her voice hadn't lost the trace of Spanish accent that had always flavored her words or its gentle tone. Now he'd grown old enough to tell it masked concern for him. Or pity? He hoped not. She squeezed his hand, and he saw that same concern in her eyes.

"Good to see you, too." He had to clear his throat before he could continue. "Both of you."

"We read about you in the newspaper. We sent you cards."

Had they? If so, he'd left them behind unread when he'd transferred from the hospital to the rehab. He would have to give her the only response he could. "I didn't write to anyone—"

"No matter. You were busy with the rodeo. And after that…" She shook her head. "You weren't well enough, we know that. The judge called the hospital for more news. That was a terrible accident. Terrible." She squeezed his fingers. "But you're well again?"

How did he answer that?

As far as his body went, yes, he was back in one piece. As "well again" as the doctors said he might ever get. But in his mind and his gut…a different story there. All those months in rehab, he'd found himself with a lot of time to think about things. To run through the memories of his life up till then.

To develop a need that wouldn't let him rest.

He couldn't tell Dori about all that.

"I'm fine," he said simply.

"And you've come home?"

He shot a glance around the café, recalling the many nights he'd swept the floors and cleared off the tables after the last customers had gone. The small, brightly decorated restaurant had once represented so much to him. A place to work, get a good meal and feel less alone. That might explain what had driven him to come in here this morning.

He'd first talked to Tess here, too. The memory caused

his stomach to clench. The fact she worked in the only real estate agency in town made their reunion inevitable. Suited his purpose, too. She'd get a firsthand look at how well he'd done for himself.

He looked back at Dori and Manny, once the only friends he'd had. Almost the only family. But…come home?

He couldn't tell Dori that, either.

"Just visiting," he said instead. "And while I'm here," he added, putting his plan into words, "I'm looking to buy some investment property."

"But that's wonderful," Dori said, obviously delighted. "You will find yourself a nice house and want to settle down here."

"I've got a house already—on a ranch in Montana." He smiled to soften the words. "But it'll be nice to visit for a while."

A short while.

Seeing Dori and Manny had revived some of the few good memories he had, but they couldn't outweigh the bad.

Once he did what he needed to do, proved he was the equal of anyone else in this town, he'd leave Flagman's Folly behind him again.

For good.

COULD ANYTHING beat showing up for work on a Monday morning and finding a long, tall cowboy waiting on the doorstep?

Yes, Tess LaSalle decided. Unfortunately, cowboys came by the dozen around here. What she needed was one with money.

It was a gorgeous first day of June, worthy of any advertising blurb she could write to attract new clients to

Wright Place Realty. But in their tiny town, there was not a client to be found.

Unless…?

Half a block away, she eyed the man leaning against the dusty pickup truck parked at the curb. From his black Stetson to his Western shirt with the shiny pearl snaps, he might have dressed to play a role. Yet one glance at his formfitting, threadbare Wranglers and well-worn black boots plainly announced the truth: he was the real thing.

Whether or not he had cash on the barrelhead remained to be seen.

Still, she hurried along Signal Street toward the store-front office. As desperately as they needed clients, she wasn't about to let this one get away.

"Good morning," she called, digging in her canvas bag for her key ring. "Let me get the office open for you."

"Morning." When she neared him, he held out his hand.

Automatically, she responded. His hand engulfed hers, the roughness of his fingers tingling all her nerve endings. She looked up to find his face hidden by the brim of his Stetson. She could see only a firm jaw and the dark stubble of five o'clock shadow. Another indication of a working cowboy and not a wealthy rancher?

As she watched, he lifted his head and tipped his hat, revealing thick, wavy dark hair and a pair of blazing green eyes.

Tess's fingers trembled in his. She'd have given anything to disappear at that moment. He couldn't have missed her reaction. Just as she couldn't miss recognizing those eyes.

Caleb Cantrell had planned that move to startle her. He'd succeeded, more than he could ever know. Shock warred with guilt inside her.

Belatedly, she realized his hand still covered hers. A

treacherous longing to hang on to him stunned her. Appalled by her own emotions, she snatched her fingers away and dropped her arm as if she'd been burned.

She took a long, deep breath and set her jaw. Forcing her voice to remain steady, she asked, "What are you doing here, Caleb?"

He gestured toward the storefront. "That's a real estate office, isn't it?"

Before she could give the obvious answer to his question, a blue van pulled up to the curb behind his pickup truck. Tess's best friend and boss, Dana Wright, emerged from the van. She did a double take at seeing Tess's companion, then marched over to them. "I don't believe my own eyes. Caleb, is that really you?"

"In the flesh."

Good-looking flesh, too, with a nice even tan that set off the whiteness of his smile as he grinned. Tess clutched the key ring she'd finally dug out of her bag.

"Well," Dana continued, "it's good to see you. You remember me? Dana Smith? Now Dana Wright?"

"Of course I remember you. Couldn't forget either of the prettiest girls in town, now could I?" He smiled at Tess.

She stiffened. He was wasting his time. No amount of sweet-talking would ever get her to believe in him again.

Sure, Dana could act natural and concerned. She didn't have Tess's history with the man.

Or Tess's secret.

"What brings you back to Flagman's Folly after all these years?" Dana asked him.

"Well, tell the truth, I'm looking to buy some land here."

"Is that so?" Dana stood taller and smiled wider.

Tess knew her friend's pulse must have quickened at

the thought of a possible sale. Her own pulse was beating fast—for other reasons.

"As we like to say around here," Dana continued, "you've come to the 'Wright Place.' I'm sure we can help you out."

"So am I. I've got a list." He tilted his head. "I'd like to talk things over with Tess. Thought we'd go on along to the Double S. Over a cup of coffee, I can fill her in on what I need."

That wasn't what *she* needed. Not at all.

She sent her friend an agonized look.

Of course, Dana couldn't understand what it meant. Instead, she sent back an expression of wide-eyed innocence that said plainly, *We'll talk later.*

"Oh, I don't think I'll be able to do much for you," Tess protested. "I'm just the hired help. A glorified file clerk, really. Dana's the boss. You'll want to deal with her."

Caleb focused on her again. "I don't know about that," he drawled. "You and I've got some catching up to do."

She curled her fingers into fists. "No, we do not, and—"

"Ahh…Tess?" Dana broke in. She looked at Caleb. "If you'll excuse us for just a minute…?"

He patted the fender of the pickup truck. "I'll be waiting right here."

"Thanks."

Within seconds, Dana had unlocked the door and led the way into the office. She turned to Tess with a wide smile—most likely for the benefit of Caleb, who stood outside the storefront window—and said, "Girl, have you completely lost your mind?"

"I don't think so."

"Well, we're *both* going to lose our jobs if we don't make a sale soon."

Tess sighed. "I know."

As a single mom and the sole breadwinner for her small family, Tess clung to the paycheck she earned here. The money took care of their bills, if she budgeted carefully. When she had pennies left, she helped tide her mother over with her fledgling business, turning their home into a bed-and-breakfast inn and taking on guests.

Nonexistent guests, lately.

Things were bad all around. No one had much money on hand for vacationing in small-town inns. Or for buying property, for that matter. Losing this job would mean she'd have no income.

Roselynn and Nate depended on her. But as bad as things were for her, she knew Dana had it much worse. Widowed and left a single mom, her friend struggled to get by with three kids of her own.

Now Dana stood tugging on a lock of her honey-brown hair, her blue eyes narrowed in speculation.

"I have no idea what all this 'catching up' is that you and Caleb have to do—" Tess remained silent "—though I'm sure I'll hear about it sometime." She smiled as if to soften the words.

Since grade school, she and Dana had shared everything. But not that. She'd never told Dana anything about her connection to Caleb. Much as Tess loved her, she knew Dana couldn't have kept herself from broadcasting the news that Tess had found a boyfriend. Tess had had her own reasons for not wanting the news spread. And after what had happened, she'd given thanks that no one had known.

"I suppose," Dana was saying, "I could offer to show him around town, but I don't want to risk him taking offense. He obviously wants to work with you."

"Yes, I know." *Why?* That's what worried her. Caleb Cantrell didn't do anything without a reason. And he certainly didn't do anything he didn't want to. She had learned that years ago. After their last conversation way back then, she couldn't imagine why he'd want to speak to her again—or how he could have the nerve to believe *she* would ever have anything to do with him.

"Look," Dana said, "I can understand your reluctance to deal with Caleb. The man didn't have such a great reputation when he lived here."

"That has nothing to do with it," she protested truthfully.

"Fine. But if there's one thing we know about him, he's made money since he left town. Who are we to keep him from spending it in Flagman's Folly? And, let's face it, we need the commission."

"I know." She couldn't refuse to work with Caleb.

Besides, did she really want Dana working with him? Talking to him? Asking him questions about that so-called "catching up" he claimed they needed to do?

"All right," she said at last, choking on the words.

But it wasn't. No matter how much money she might bring in by making a sale for Wright Place Realty, dealing with Caleb Cantrell could cost her plenty. If he ever found out about the baby she'd kept from him, it might cost her the daughter she loved.

Chapter Two

"Now you know what I'm looking for," Caleb finished up. Across their booth in the Double S, Tess stared down at her notebook. "The best money can buy."

He had grabbed his coffee and her tea and headed to the empty booth at the far front corner of the room, close to the café's door. Not that he would need a getaway...

Tess didn't look too happy about sitting here with him. And she'd said next to nothing, leaving him to spend the last half hour doing enough talking to make his throat drier than New Mexico dust. Luckily, Dori kept the pot hot and full.

He glanced down at the woven place mat under his coffee mug, then around the room at the rough wooden tables and chairs, the bare planked floors, the colorful sombreros on the wall.

At anything that gave him the chance to think for a minute without staring at Tess.

Why he should find it hard to look her in the eye, he didn't know. Finding out she worked selling real estate had given him the best reason in the world for getting in touch with her once he'd come back to town. And her job made her just the person he needed to get his point across to everyone. He'd run down a list a mile long, throwing in every option he could think of for the kind of property he wanted to buy. The best, the biggest. The most expensive property.

He looked around the café. At this hour, too late for workers to stop in for coffees to go and too early for a lunch rush, the restaurant had only a few customers. Luckily, no one he knew. He'd returned to Flagman's Folly eager to get to work, but now that he had arrived, he'd realized he should've done more thinking beforehand about his great idea.

Much as he hated to admit it, seeing Tess again had shaken him more than he would have guessed.

But it was time to put his plan into action.

He looked back at her. "You got all that?"

"I believe so." Her head down, she flipped back through the pages of the notebook that lay on the table beside her.

He took the opportunity to check her out yet again.

Could have knocked him over with a frayed lasso when he'd seen her come walking along Signal Street. Luckily he'd gotten hold of himself by the time she'd reached him.

During the past ten years, Tess hadn't changed a bit.

Well...naturally, she'd grown up and filled out.

Still, she had the same shoulder-length tumble of dark curls, the pale skin that gave her away every time she blushed, the sparkling dark brown eyes. She looked up at him again now, those eyes wide, and said not a word.

He glanced down to see her hanging on to her teacup for dear life, it seemed. No wedding band. He wondered about that.

Not that it meant anything to him.

If only he could say the same about the way her fingers had trembled in his when he'd shaken her hand earlier...

Letting go of the death grip on her cup, she transferred her attention to the hem of her yellow shirt. The tug she gave on it pulled the fabric taut against her.

He forced himself to focus on taking a long swallow of his coffee.

"I think I've got everything we'll need." Her lips curved briefly. "Any last-minute items for your wish list?"

Yeah. A real smile. That one had looked so fake, he wouldn't have given her a nickel for it. "Nope. That about covers it for now."

"Then I'll get back to the office and start working on this. I'm sure we'll be able to find something to suit you." She flipped the notebook closed and dropped it into her bag.

When she started to slide out from the booth, he reached for her arm. Warm, soft skin met his palm. Holding her hand outside the office had given him a jolt. This about mule-kicked him across the room.

He pulled his hand away and cleared his throat. "What's your hurry? Been a long time since the two of us talked."

"Yes."

Obviously, if she had her way, it would be an even longer time before they had a proper conversation.

He settled against his seat cushions and stretched his legs out under the table, trying to find a comfortable position. "So, you wound up selling property for a living? Not a bad job. What does your husband do?"

And why the heck had he asked that?

Tess looked as if she wondered the same thing. "I don't have a husband," she said, clipping the words.

He frowned. "Last time I saw you, you were planning on getting married."

"I know," she said, her voice cold. "It didn't work out."

"Yeah. Neither did we." Again, he'd blurted the response without thinking. This time, though, he knew why. The bitter memory of their last meeting had driven him to speech.

He might as well have waved a red flag in front of her with his words. Her face went as belligerent as a bull getting ready to charge.

"There was no 'we,' Caleb. I seem to remember that maybe once there might have been. But *you* wanted to go off and start winding your way along the rodeo trail. So you did."

The acid in her tone seemed at odds with the hurt look in her eyes.

Well, he'd had his reasons. And she'd damned well given him another. One guaranteed to keep him away. Jaw clenched, he tried shrugging away the wave of guilt pounding at him. No such luck. He reached for the fresh pot of coffee Dori had brought a few minutes back.

The door to the Double S opened. Glad for the distraction, he looked up and watched a group of little girls roll like tumbleweeds into the place.

On the opposite side of the booth, Tess jerked to attention. He'd swear her face grew paler yet.

"Anything wrong?" he asked.

She shook her head.

She was lying. Something about that little crowd bothered her.

"Excuse me a minute," she said.

The girls had crossed the café and taken over the row of stools lining the counter in the back of the room. They looked innocent enough. Clean and respectable, too. A big contrast to the kid he'd given the cash to earlier.

The same thing people had thought about him when he'd lived here. He gripped the handle of his coffee mug, trying to get hold of his anger. At that age, neither he nor that kid had the power to control their worlds. Couldn't folks understand that?

He shook his head and looked again at the girls. Eight,

nine years old, maybe. He'd seen plenty like them in his days on the circuit. Just a bunch of giggling kids who cared only about hanging out at the rodeo with their friends. Nothing to worry about with girls that age.

It was the older ones you had to watch out for.

Eyes half-closed, he sat back and admired the view of Tess's yellow shirt riding above well-fitting khakis as she marched toward the group of girls.

When she came up to them, they swung around on their stools. The sideways glances the four of them shot each other said plainly they hadn't expected to run into her here.

She leaned close to one of the kids, a pint-size version of Tess with dark curls and a stubborn chin he'd recognized easily. Had to be Tess's little girl.

All the coffee he'd swallowed that morning suddenly churned in his stomach.

The kid stuck that chin out now and shook her head. Then she crossed her arms over her chest and turned away from Tess. Trouble there, for sure.

The girl looked around the room at anyone and anything but her mama. Her gaze zeroed in on him, and her eyes widened to about the size of his competition champion belt buckles.

"Mom, look!" she said in a strangled whisper. She might've been trying to keep her voice down, but he could hear her clear across the room. She tugged on Tess's shirt. "Mom, do you *see* him?" Her voice rose with every word. She waved her arms frantically at her friends. "Guys— over there, in the corner. That's *Caleb Cantrell.*"

The trio surrounding her squealed like a sty full of pigs discovering a replenished trough. A familiar enough sound.

He smiled in satisfaction. Now, this was one group in Flagman's Folly he wouldn't need to work at impressing.

All four of them jumped off their stools.

To give her credit, Tess made an attempt to grab hold of her daughter and the girl next to her. They likely didn't even feel her hands on their shoulders as they slipped from her grasp. At that moment they were driven, with one goal in mind.

Getting to him.

From the look on Tess's face, she wanted to be anywhere but here.

Carefully, he set his half-full coffee mug aside, moved his Stetson out of reach and braced himself, knowing what would happen next.

The girls headed toward him. No tumbleweeds rolling gently along now. Their eyes shining, their mouths tight with suppressed excitement, they stampeded across the room.

"ALL RIGHT." Tess looked from one girl to another, stopping at Nate. "You remember that list of chores you promised to do for Miss Roselynn in exchange for the sleepover tonight?"

They all nodded.

"Well, that's a start." She had spent more time than she could afford trying to drag their attention away from Caleb.

As rodeo-crazy as Nate and her friends were, she should have known Nate would recognize the champion bull rider immediately. If only the girls hadn't come into the Double S just when she happened to be there with Caleb. But that was a faint if only—and a useless one. In a town the size of Flagman's Folly, *everyone* would run into him sooner than later.

In the minute it took for those thoughts to flash through her mind, the girls had edged closer to Caleb again.

She tensed. "Get started now, girls," she said. "Miss Roselynn will be waiting for those groceries."

Even to her own ears, she'd sounded as firm as a blade of wet grass. Looking across the booth at Caleb, she felt just about as sturdy. After this run-in with him, she really needed peace and quiet. And time to practice the calm front she would have to present whenever he was around.

But there wasn't time enough in the world for that.

Besides, the way he sat smiling at her left no doubt he'd noticed her staring at him. He'd probably already seen right through her. As bad as the girls, she now had to drag her own attention away from the man, who obviously had plenty of experience in the spotlight.

"You've got the list for Harley's," she reminded Nate and her friends. "And you've got the money, too?" At their nods, she added, "Great. Then please get the shopping done—and don't forget to use the coupons."

Every penny saved meant a penny more she could use to help her mother put food on the tables at the bed-and-breakfast. The Whistlestop Inn might be empty of guests now, but with any luck, Roselynn would soon have every room occupied. And not by a houseful of chattering girls.

That was all she needed tonight.

After a burst of giggles and goodbyes to Caleb, the group ran toward the door.

One voice rose above the laughter. "'Bye, Mom. See ya later." The door slammed in her wake.

Tess sank back onto the booth's bench seat.

"Sleepover?" he asked.

"They're celebrating school letting out last week." She exhaled heavily. With the way Nate had behaved lately, she'd skated very close to *not* having this party. And if things didn't improve, it could turn into a very long summer.

The thought that Caleb might be there for a good part of it left her choking on her indrawn breath of dismay. She swore she'd do whatever it took to have him on his way as soon as possible. Focusing on him again, she realized she'd missed the beginning of his response.

"—can't be a bad bunch at all," he was saying, "if they're willing to do chores that cheerfully. And your daughter sure takes after you."

The blood seemed to rush from her head, making her dizzy. There were many subjects she never, ever wanted to discuss with Caleb Cantrell. On a scale of zero to ten, the topic of her daughter ranked at three hundred.

"Yes," she said shortly. She shoved one shaking hand through her hair. With the other, she picked up her canvas bag as she rose from the bench. "Well, I've got your information. Time for me to go and start working on it."

She turned away and waved a brief goodbye to Dori. The older woman stood with her elbows resting on the counter at the back of the room, taking a much-needed break.

"You'll come see us again soon?" Dori asked, directing the question to Tess but then quickly looking past her toward Caleb.

Was *no* female over the age of five immune to the man's charms?

"I'm sure *I* will," Tess said firmly.

"Be a real pleasure, Dori," he drawled. "For both of us."

Tess shivered and grabbed the door handle. She didn't want to share *any* kind of pleasure with him. Not now or in the future. And she refused even to think about their past.

Once outside, she stopped on the sidewalk near his pickup truck. He had driven them the couple of blocks to the Double S, and the close confines of the truck's cab had nearly left her hyperventilating. The two blocks had stretched to forty miles.

No way did she want to share that vehicle with him again, either.

"So," he said, resting against the fender, just as he'd been standing when she had first seen him that morning. "How old is she?"

"Dori?" She pretended to misunderstand, knowing full well what he meant. "I'm not sure. Around my mother's age, I would guess. Early sixties."

The deception hurt her. Badly. Because at her response, he grinned, making his green eyes blaze even in the shadow beneath his Stetson's brim. "I meant that girl of yours."

"Oh. She's nine."

"Nice-looking kid. What's her name?"

"N-Nate." Where was he going with this conversation? And why wasn't *she* going far, far away in another direction?

"Nate?" He sounded amused. "A real handful."

She frowned. He'd seen her daughter for all of five minutes, most of which Nate had spent amid the group of girls fawning over him. "What makes you say that?"

"The stubborn jaw." He reached up and touched her chin with his fingertip. "I'd have known her even if she didn't have your hair."

She swallowed hard and backed up a step, her legs threatening to give way beneath her. No, she would not get back in that pickup truck with him—even though it would give her a chance to sit down.

"I'll be in touch," she assured him. *When cows give orange milk.* "I'm sure it won't take long at all. And..." she held her breath a moment, then rushed on "I'm assuming you've reserved a place to stay closer to Santa Fe or Albuquerque."

His expression hardened. "I've got it covered," he said, his voice rough.

At another time, she might have thought twice about his reaction. Not anymore. "Good," she said firmly. "There's no need for you to hang around. I have your cell phone number. And you don't need to drive me to the office, thanks."

As she started along the sidewalk, he fell into step beside her. Though he matched his stride to hers, he walked with the stiff gait she had seen when he'd first gotten out of the truck in front of the Double S.

He'd been hurt during a rodeo. Very seriously hurt. The townsfolk had gone into an uproar when they'd learned about it. Nate and her friends had been despondent. Tess had managed to harden her heart against the news. Had tried not to think about Caleb's aborted career. About his injury. For the most part, she'd succeeded. Until now.

Reading about his accident was one thing. Seeing the results of it right there in front of her was something else. But she couldn't feel any pity for Caleb. Shouldn't feel any guilt, either.

Not after they way he had crushed her.

Keeping her gaze forward, she cleared her throat. "I— uh—know the way back on my own."

"That's good," he said. "A successful real estate person like yourself ought to know her way around. In fact, I imagine you're the perfect person to show me some of the sights in town."

Shaky legs or not, that brought her to a solid stop. "What are you playing at, Caleb? You were born and raised here, same as I was. You know all the sights there are to see."

"Maybe. And maybe some things have changed."

His gaze drifted from her eyes all the way to her toes. An answering shiver rippled its way along the same path, as if he'd run his finger down her body.

"You've got more curves than I remember." He grinned again.

Time to get away from him. "I have to run." *What an understatement.*

She needed to get to her office, research the list of his requirements, and find some property for him as quickly as she could—and as far away from Flagman's Folly as possible.

"Okay." To her relief, he nodded. "Tell you what. I've got some business to take care of, myself. Since yours won't take long, why don't I pick you up later? We'll ride around town a bit. Talk over your prospects at supper."

The most *un*likely prospect she'd ever heard.

The words rested on the tip of her tongue, ready for her to say them. But she couldn't.

Visions floated into her mind.

Nate. Roselynn. Dana with her three small children but no husband by her side. An Out Of Business notice plastered on the front window of Wright Place Realty. A For Sale sign decorating the lawn of the Whistlestop Inn.

She thought of the commissions she and Dana would earn from the sale of a ranch to Caleb. The sale of a *substantial* ranch. He'd made it plain he intended to acquire the largest piece of property she could locate. He'd seemed obsessed by the idea of owning a big spread in New Mexico. Strange, when he'd told her he already ran a working ranch in Montana. She'd had to bite her tongue against the question she wanted to ask. Why did he feel such a need to branch out?

Fortunately, she'd kept quiet. What did it matter to her,

as long as she managed to find him that ranch clear across the state? She ought to be grateful for his obsession. The income she could earn in satisfying his need would take care of every worry she'd envisioned, for a good long time. She couldn't afford—literally—to get on the man's bad side.

If he had one.

Everything she'd seen of him so far looked as good if not better than it had ten years ago.

"Sound all right to you?" he persisted. "You said you're still living at your mama's. Can she keep watch on the girls at the sleepover for a while?"

She swallowed hard. "Yes, she can. That sounds fine."

"Good. I'll be at your place early, then, around four."

She nodded and walked away before he could see the expression she knew she couldn't hide.

How many times as a love-struck teenager had she dreamed about Caleb pulling up to the house to pick her up for a date? Impossible, of course. Her grandfather had made sure of it. Even without Granddad's rules, she had known the pointlessness of her dream. She and Caleb had kept their relationship secret.

She sighed in frustration.

Back then, she had loved Caleb. Couldn't get enough of him. Yet he had left her. And now, when she didn't want the man anywhere near her, she was stuck with him.

The irony of the situation nearly overwhelmed her. But the damage was done. Her world had already caved in earlier that day, the minute he had forced his way into her life again.

Chapter Three

Caleb parked the pickup truck in his choice of spaces behind Tess's home. Only one other vehicle occupied the parking area, an ancient Toyota with more than its share of dents.

Funny to think he'd come calling here again. Twice in the past, he'd stopped by this place and hadn't made it beyond the front door. Her granddaddy had seen to that. Getting inside now would bring him a considerable measure of satisfaction.

Still, anger rose at the memory of her granddaddy. The same anger that had bubbled through his veins since he'd first set foot in town this morning. He'd have to watch that. Control that from here on. Anger wouldn't get him what he wanted from the townsfolk, or from Tess. No, he needed to give them all someone to look up to. Someone they'd respect.

A good storyteller. A bull-riding champ. A rodeo star.

Taking a deep breath, he stared at the clock on the dashboard. Three-fifty. Ten minutes early. Ten minutes to sit here. No sense letting Tess think he was too eager to see her again.

He couldn't have any illusions about her feelings, that was for sure.

She had looked less than thrilled to see him outside

the real estate office that morning, and a good sight more unhappy once she learned why he'd been standing on the doorstep.

What he'd told her of his reasons, anyhow.

Pity she hadn't been more enthused.

As if she would forget about their past, just because he'd wanted her to. As if he could impress her, just by mentioning money. He'd known he would have to work harder with Tess than with anyone. Maybe he should have started with somebody who'd have accepted his return more readily.

Dori and Manny from the Double S, for instance.

Of everyone in Flagman's Folly, they were the people he should have harbored some guilt over. Maybe he did, somewhere deep inside. Someplace he couldn't get to right now. Not while he had grudges to tackle and axes to grind and scores to settle. He had all the bad parts of his past to resolve before he could look to the future.

Coming to the edge of dying had made him realize that. It had humbled him. It had scared the hell out of him. And it had finally made him understand just what all those early years and those bad parts of his past had done to him.

Returning to Flagman's Folly had to make up for some of that.

He glanced at the dashboard clock again. Time for the show to begin.

He climbed out of the truck and followed the path around the house to the front door. When he had driven by earlier that day, he'd seen the small sign near the sidewalk, proclaiming this the Whistlestop Inn. The sight had surprised him. Another thing that had changed since he'd left town.

Always, he had envied Tess this old house with its two stories, peaked roof and deep porch corralled by rails. A wooden-slatted swing dangled from chains in the porch ceiling. He'd always wanted to sit in that swing, too. It overlooked rows of plants with big pink and yellow and orange blooms and the yard that ran down to the street.

The porch alone took up more footage than that piece of crap trailer he'd lived in growing up.

He stabbed the doorbell and stepped back. Inside the house, he heard chimes, followed by some screeching and a lot of loud laughter. The girls, again.

Smiling, he shook his head. Kids were the same everywhere. Grown-up fans were, too. The autographs he'd signed all across the country proved that.

Abruptly the inner door swung open. Through the screened door, Tess's dark-brown eyes stared at him from a pint-size height. The kid could almost have passed as Tess's double. In a few years, grown up, she no doubt would. She'd look amazingly like the Tess he'd left behind.

Now those eyes rounded like the mouth beneath it.

"Better watch it, kid," he said. "Didn't your mama ever tell you your face might freeze that way?"

Her features went slack. "Yeah, all the time." She grinned. "My name's not kid, Mr. Cantrell. It's Nate."

"So I heard. And my name's Caleb."

She sucked in a breath. "You mean I can call you that?"

He nodded.

"Wow."

There went the eyes again. He chuckled. "What's the deal, if you don't mind my asking? Nate's a boy's name, isn't it?"

"Yeah." She looked down, suddenly shy, the dark curls falling to hide most of her face.

He couldn't help it. The urge came on him strong to tease her, just as he'd kidded her mama years ago, though Tess had been older then. "Can't be your real name," he said. "Come on, give."

She paused, considering him for a moment, then stared at her feet. "Anastasia," she hissed, her tone disgusted. She peeked out from under all that hair to see how he was taking the news.

"Hmm." He nodded thoughtfully. Now that he'd gotten himself into this, how should he handle it? "Well. Sounds like a right pretty name to me."

"It *does?*" She looked straight at him again. "Nobody has that name but me."

"That makes it pretty *and* special, then, doesn't it?"

"I don't know." Shrugging, she rubbed the toe of one shoe against the floor. "Ya coming in, or are ya just ringing doorbells for fun?"

He had to chomp down for a second on the corner of his lip before he could answer. "Is it fun?"

"Yeah. If nobody catches you."

"Hmm," he said again. "Well…" So far, he wouldn't take any prizes for his conversational skills. Hopefully, he'd have more luck with Tess later. But if he wasn't talking horses or rodeo, he sure felt at a loss when it came to kids. How could he answer this one? "Considering I did get caught ringing your bell," he said slowly, "and by you…I'll have to confess I was planning on coming in."

"*Really?* C'mon." She pushed open the screened door to let him in, then she turned and raced through the foyer. "Hey, guys," she yelled at a level that could quiet an arena without a bullhorn. "You won't believe who's here!"

He stepped into the foyer.

And found Tess staring at him.

She looked good in a tight-fitting Western shirt, almost a twin to his own, but more feminine in pink with a rose at each shoulder. He couldn't resist getting a full look at her snug jeans and brown cowboy boots.

Eventually, he worked his way up again to confront her

unblinking gaze. He had frozen in the act of removing his Stetson. *Dang*. He was here to impress the woman, not stand gawking at her. Hurriedly, he swept his arm across his waist and bowed. "Well, hey. Didn't see you standing there, ma'am." He gestured between them. "The way we're dressed, we might almost be related."

Her mouth taut, she said nothing.

He frowned. "Aren't you going to welcome me in?"

She took a deep breath and let it out in an exasperated sigh. "I think someone already did."

Conscious of Caleb behind her, Tess hurried across the foyer and into the dining room. She had deliberately steered him away from the opposite side of the house, where Nate and her friends had claimed the living room. That was the last place she wanted him to go, and Nate was the last person she wanted him to see.

"Why don't we take a look at what I've pulled together," she said over her shoulder, "and then we can be on our way."

Or with luck, Caleb could leave on his own.

If she took care of all their business here and now, they might skip going out altogether. And if that didn't work, maybe she could at least avoid a tour of the town with him until absolutely necessary.

Still shaken by his greeting, she plopped down into a chair at the long central dining table and waved at the empty seats. Her briefcase rested on the chair beside hers, where she felt thankful to have it as a barricade. "I didn't expect you to stop in," she said. "I thought we would just hit the road."

Let him think she hadn't a worry in the world about going out alone with him.

"Seems like your daughter had different ideas. *She's* got the notion of Southern hospitality down pat."

She froze, a file folder half out of her case. "Meaning, I haven't?"

He considered. "Your welcome was on the cold side, wouldn't you say?"

"I'm not used to having people in my home, uninvited." That was rude. And so untrue. Sort of.

"Thought we settled the invitation part of it." He eyed the smaller tables scattered in various parts of the room. "And looks to me like you're used to feeding a herd. I saw the sign outside. How's business?"

"Fine. But it's not my concern." He'd sounded surprised about the house's transformation and looked at her now with his eyebrows raised. "My mother owns the bed-and-breakfast. I just happen to live here."

"With Nate."

"Yes, of course, with Nate." She fought not to grind her teeth.

"And with your mother, of course. And your grand-daddy."

"No, my grandfather passed away a couple of years ago." She had no idea why he would care, but he seemed oddly surprised by the news.

"Well," he said, "surely you know if there are guests around the house or not."

She shrugged. "I'm too busy working to pay much attention."

"The real estate business keeps you hopping, huh? Never would have thought that, myself." He gave her a piercing glance. "Guess I was right—things have changed around town."

An even more touchy subject. "*Some* things," she said tightly. Years ago, she could never have let him into this house. Would never have been able to face the consequences. She only wished he wasn't here now. Part of her did, anyway.

Another part of her felt remorse. For Nate's sake, she wished she could be nicer to him, could forgive him for the past. At the thought, she hardened her heart. Would Caleb feel any remorse for the way he had treated her?

"How many years has it been?" he asked. "About nine? Ten?"

With his questions, all thoughts of forgiveness fled her mind.

"About," she muttered. She could tell him how long it had been since they'd last seen each other, down to the day. To the hour.

She folded her arms across her chest as if that could protect her. Too late. His questions had already triggered a whole list of thoughts she wanted—needed—to stay away from.

"This place never was an inn before," he said thoughtfully. "What made your mother go into business for herself?"

"As I told you, my grandfather died. He left the house to her, and she decided to start the bed-and-breakfast." Short and sweet and all he needed to know. She needed to get him out of here. "Now, if you don't mind, we'll concentrate on *your* business. I've got—"

Nate and her friends rushed into the room, their sneakers screeching on the polished floor as the girls skidded to a stop beside the table.

Tess's heart sank.

"Caleb—" Nate shot a glance at Tess. "He said I can call him that, Mom." She turned back. "Can you stay and have supper with us?"

"No, I don't think—" Tess began.

"C'mon, Caleb," Nate urged, her unblinking gaze on him showing she obviously hadn't even heard Tess's words. "We're having a sleepover. We're gonna grill hot dogs and burgers, and Gram's making potato salad."

"Yes, I am. The best red-potato salad you'll find this side of the Mississippi."

At the sound of her mother's voice, Tess swallowed a groan and looked across the room.

Just inside the doorway stood Roselynn and Aunt Ella-mae, wearing smiles as alike as rows of kernels on a corn-cob. Tess eyed them warily. With those two, you could never know what to expect next. Just like Nate, as a matter of fact. "Caleb and I have some paperwork to take care of," she told them.

"Oh, sugar." Southern sweetness dripped from Rose-lynn's words. "You worked hard all day. Surely that can wait."

"Yeah," Ellamae added. "At least till after the fresh-made pecan pie."

Caleb grinned, and he glanced from one eager face to another—all six of them. With great effort, only Tess kept her expression carefully neutral.

"Ladies," he said, "I don't see how I can rightly refuse an invitation like that one."

Nate took him by the hand, and he rose to his feet.

Tess's eyes stung. Her heart sank even lower.

"C'mon," her daughter said. "Let's go out back by the grill." As she led him away, she added in a hoarse whisper, "Maybe you can do the burgers. Mom always burns 'em."

The rest of the girls followed in their wake like a row of baby ducklings behind their daddy and mama.

Her own mother and aunt looked at her, looked at

each other, still beaming, and then disappeared from the doorway.

Tess put her elbows on the table and her head into her hands.

This couldn't be happening. It just couldn't. After almost a decade, Caleb couldn't be back here again.

But he was. Talking about the past and the changes around here and how many years it had been. If it ever occurred to him to sit down and do the math…

That couldn't happen, either.

Tess shot to her feet. Determination propelled her across the dining room. She had to get that man out of her house. Had to make sure he never set foot in it again.

Most of all, she had to keep him from ever finding out that Nate—her horse-crazy, rodeo-loving, rebellious daughter Nate—was his daughter, too.

Chapter Four

The evening couldn't have gotten any worse, from Tess's perspective. She curled up on her lawn chair in the shadowy backyard and tried not to groan.

With the burgers and hot dogs and potato salad long gone, supper had given way to the night's entertainment.

Caleb.

He'd started in on tales of his life on the rodeo circuit, as if they had all come together to share stories over a cozy little campfire. Next thing she knew, they'd be toasting marshmallows over the grill and singing "Kumbaya."

Sighing, she wrapped her arms around her upraised knees.

Nate and the rest of the girls sat cross-legged at Caleb's feet. They stared up at him, their openmouthed looks of hero worship obvious for everyone to see. Even Roselynn and Ellamae had drawn their chairs over to the group, the better to hear his low drawl.

Traitors.

Yet, how could she blame them? Hadn't he roped her in, too, just with different kinds of stories? Not anymore, though. Never again.

"How did you ever get out of that field?" asked Lissa Wright, Dana's oldest child and Nate's best friend.

"Didn't that bull kill you?" another of the girls asked.

Nate rolled her eyes. "Of course not, silly. He's here, isn't he? Right, Caleb?"

"Right."

Even from across the yard, Tess could see him struggling to keep from laughing.

"As for how I got out of there, it's like this." With every word his voice grew more animated, holding the girls enthralled. "I whipped off my bandana and blindfolded that bull so fast, he didn't know what hit him. Got him so confused, he ran into a fence post harder than his own head. The darned fool knocked himself out."

Her Aunt Ellamae, always given to plain speaking, responded with a very unladylike snort. "Caleb Cantrell, that's a lot of bull, and you know it."

He grinned at her. "He sure was, ma'am."

Aunt El laughed.

Tess gave in to the groan she'd tried so hard to hold back and put her chin on her knees.

"Mom," Nate called, starry-eyed in the lamps' glow, "are you listening to all this?"

"I don't know if I'm hearing it just right," she said, forcing enthusiasm into her voice. "It sounds almost too good to be true."

The *real* truth was, except for the most exciting moments during his stories, when either Caleb raised his voice or the girls repeated in awestruck tones something he'd said, she hadn't heard anything at all. From her seat, Caleb's words came as a murmur. A low, sexy murmur. As much as the sound unsteadied her, she preferred not being able to hear him clearly.

Why would she want to know the details of the bait that had lured him away from her?

In the brief moment when everyone had turned to look at Tess, Caleb stared at her. His eyes shone as bright as

Nate's. Not with the glint of excitement, though. Those eyes, his solemn expression, his stiff shoulders, all showed he had caught the false enthusiasm in her tone.

It seemed to bother him. She didn't understand why. But she didn't care.

"What's the biggest rodeo you were ever in?" Lissa asked.

"Well, let me think…"

Caleb broke eye contact with Tess, the audience focused on their star again, and Tess let her attention turn inward.

She knew nothing about Caleb's biggest rodeo, but she would never forget his *first* one….

She'd known nothing about his dreams, either, when they'd first found each other in high school. Two lonely teenagers, they'd held on tight to a relationship made even more precious because it was theirs alone.

Their secret.

Yet a few months later, Caleb had left town—left *her*—to go off on the rodeo trail. When she didn't hear from him right away, she told herself not to worry. He had sworn he would call. He would write.

When the weeks went by without a word, it grew harder for her to believe in his empty promises.

And when two months had passed and she'd discovered she was pregnant, she'd had nowhere to turn. She couldn't tell her mom. She'd die before she would confess to Aunt El. And wouldn't survive if Granddad ever found out.

She couldn't even risk telling her best friend, Dana.

She *had* to find Caleb.

And she did.

After weeks of online searches, she had finally tracked him down at a rodeo outside Gallup. She'd had to use most of her babysitting money to buy a round-trip bus ticket that would take her there and back the same day.

She had arrived at the arena just in time to find Caleb flushed with success at his first major win—and with two girls wrapped around him. One giggled into his ear while the other one planted a lipstick-stained kiss on his cheek.

Her own cheeks flaming, Tess had approached the trio.

At first, Caleb looked as though he would deny knowing her. Then, he simply denied that he had any interest in her—by turning to walk away.

She stopped him, saying she had something important to discuss.

"Time to collect my prize," he told her. "Come and watch, Tess. *That's* what's important. That's what will save me from going back to some one-horse town with one-horse folks in it."

Obviously, his statement included her.

Raising her jaw, she stared him down. Sheer willpower kept her from telling him how he'd made her feel. She'd never in her life been so hurt. So humiliated.

Stubborn pride prevented her from telling him about the baby. Instead, she blurted out the news she was getting married.

That didn't interest him, either. He'd stood there, not saying a word, the silence hanging between them until, finally, he'd wished her well.

Best of luck, he'd said. Damn him.

Then they'd shouted his name over the loudspeakers, and even before he'd turned his lipstick-stained face from her, before he'd rushed off to claim his all-important prize, her heart had broken.

By the time she had walked away, she'd promised herself Caleb Cantrell would never know what he'd meant to her. And he would never know about their child....

In the glow of the hurricane lamp on the picnic table, someone moved toward her. She jumped. Gone so deeply into her thoughts, wrapped so completely in memories, she hadn't noticed anyone approaching. She looked up to see Caleb standing in front of her. It took her a long, startled moment to come to her senses.

When she did, she shot a glance past him, to find they were alone in the backyard.

She tried to rise from her lawn chair. Her legs, curled in one position for who knew how long, almost gave way. Staggering slightly, she managed to catch herself. Caleb didn't seem to notice. Still, to her dismay, she imagined him reaching out to steady her. Could almost feel the heat from his hands washing through her, as cozy and warm as if she *had* been sitting all that time in front of the camp-fire she'd thought about. She felt an overwhelming desire to move closer, to have him wrap his arms around her.

Was she crazy? Shaking her head at her own stupidity, she eased away from him.

She'd been burned by Caleb once. Hadn't that been enough?

Hoping her stiff legs would bear her weight, she moved aside and rested her hip against the nearest picnic table.

"Nice meal," he said.

She nodded.

"Still got that pecan pie to go."

"Yes."

"Good company, too. But you didn't seem to feel much like joining in the conversation."

What could she say in response? Nothing Caleb would want to hear. She shrugged, hoping he would leave it at that.

He didn't. Of course.

"Not into rodeo?" he asked.

Astonished, she stared at him. Could he really have asked that question? Could he have forgotten what happened the one and only time they'd been together at a rodeo? Or worse, did he not even care? She swallowed a bitter laugh. He didn't care at all. Of course.

Why should she? "I was at a rodeo with you, Caleb. Or I should say, I followed you to one. Once."

"Yeah, that's right." He tucked his thumbs into his belt loops. Not meeting her eyes, he said, "Sorry about that night."

She shook her head again, this time in stunned disbelief. He'd tossed out the offhanded apology with as much care as he'd tossed paper plates into the trash after their supper.

"It doesn't matter," she said. "That one time was enough for me. I never had much interest in going to rodeos after that."

"Look, I guess I got caught up in the win and wanted more."

"More what? Fame and fortune?" Not more time with her. "You got that, didn't you? And the stories to go with it." She couldn't resist adding, "But then, the rodeo didn't teach you that. You always talked a good line."

"Tess—"

She raised her hand to cut him off. "Sorry, I shouldn't have said that." Shouldn't have wasted her breath. At least *her* apology had held some sincerity.

Caleb hadn't changed, and she'd been foolish to think he might have. Even more foolish to hope she could ever feel close to him again. "Tell you what. Let's just leave the past in the past, where it belongs. It's history."

"Yeah, but you're part of my history. And I'm part of yours. No getting away from that."

No, she couldn't ever forget it. If he only knew how big a role their past played in her life every day...

A cold chill running through her now, she wrapped her arms around her waist, missing the warmth she'd so recently felt. "I don't know where you're planning to go with that, Caleb, but you can just stop right there. I won't have any more interest in your story than I did in your rodeo tales." She forced herself to stand straight again, abandoning the support of the picnic table. Then she steeled herself to look up at him. "Yes, I'm part of your history," she agreed. "The part you left behind."

EVEN THOUGH he now had his mind and hands occupied with two fistfuls' worth of playing cards, Caleb had plenty of focus left to dwell on the conversation he'd just had with Tess.

Or *tried* to have, more like it. She hadn't listened to what he'd already said and wouldn't let him get another word in edgewise. He had heard the hurt in her voice and knew part of him deserved the words she'd flung at him. Still, they'd stung.

He'd have protested, would have spoken up in his own defense, if her pint-size daughter hadn't returned to the backyard to lead him away and into the dining room, where the other girls had gathered around the long table.

Tess eventually joined them. Reluctantly, he could tell. He had to fight not to crush the cards in his fist.

Yeah, dammit, he'd left her behind. But he'd meant to come back. He'd sworn it. Only things hadn't worked out that way. Life never did go the way you had it planned. Tess ought to know that. Hadn't she said as much herself when she'd told him about her marriage not working out?

Besides, she'd come to him first. To deliver her good news.

Slowly, he loosened his grip on the cards. He looked

around the dining room again at the scattering of small tables he'd seen earlier, when he'd first arrived and she had brought him into this room. She'd cut him off quick when he'd asked her about business.

She'd lied, too, saying things were fine.

When Nate had taken him to the back of the yard to get more charcoal for the grill, he'd seen the worn-out condition of the shed there and the broken-down fence sagging behind it. When he and the girls had put the card game on hold to rearrange the living room furniture for the sleepover, he'd seen the frayed edge of carpet behind the couch. Roselynn's business wasn't fine, and he knew it. He'd also bet real estate didn't keep Tess as busy as she'd let on.

He would eat this handful of cards if she could prove either of those things to him otherwise.

Well, if she wouldn't give him the truth, he would get it somewhere else.

She'd just headed into the kitchen to put the teakettle on.

He threw his leftover cards onto the pile on the table. While one of the girls shuffled the deck, he rose to straddle his chair backward, tilting it on its rear legs, moving closer to a small table for two placed against one dining room wall.

Roselynn and Ellamae sat there, polishing off a couple of pieces of Ellamae's pie. Roselynn turned her attention to him.

"Caleb, may I cut you another slice?"

He nodded. "Just a sliver."

When she handed it to him, he took a forkful, smiled his appreciation, then said, "The bed-and-breakfast here is new since my time. How long have you had it running?"

"Just a year now."

"Things going well?"

A slight wrinkle appeared between her brows and she fussed with the pie server. She didn't have Tess's flair for avoiding answers, though. "Fair to middlin', I guess," she said finally.

Ellamae made a choking sound. "Roselynn, your nose is gonna grow. Fact is," she said to Caleb, "the inn business is almost out the window."

"No guests?"

"No guests."

"We've had a few," Roselynn protested. Then she sighed. "But not for a long spell."

He couldn't state the obvious, that Flagman's Folly didn't have enough going for it to make it a tourist attraction. She'd have to do something to draw them in. "Are you advertising?" he asked.

"That's expensive."

"True. But as people say, sometimes you've got to spend money to make money."

"I suppose you're right." Roselynn lifted the empty pie plate. "Excuse me. I'll just run this into the kitchen."

When she'd gone, Ellamae chuckled. "*Run's* the word, all right. Looks like you've just scared her off. Not something you're used to with women, I'd reckon."

"They're usually headed in my direction," he acknowledged. "Used to be, anyhow."

"What happened?"

He blinked.

"Yeah, I know," she said. "I'm nosy. And I'm blunt. You ought to remember that from days past."

"I sure do." He laughed.

She was tough, too, and wiry, an older woman with gray-

ing hair and snapping dark eyes. Looked like any number
of seasoned cowhands he could name. But Ellamae didn't
herd cattle. She had an even more demanding job.

Keeping the peace in this town.

Ellamae worked as the court clerk. As a teen, Caleb had
been up at the judge's bench a time or two, called in for
jaywalking and riding with no lights on his bike—minor
offenses not regularly requiring a court appearance. But
in Flagman's Folly, things didn't always run the "regular"
way. Another reason he'd left town at the first opportunity
and never come back. Until today.

Judge Baylor kept a firm grip on his gavel inside the
courtroom *and* out. And Caleb had always suspected Ellamae, with her direct way of dealing with folks, held as
much power as the judge when it came to anything that
went on around here.

Maybe that's why she'd unbent once in a while and let
him off the hook when the judge cracked down on him.
Maybe it's why she was conversing so freely with him
tonight. And why he somehow felt he could trust her in
return.

"We could use some straight talking right now," he
said, thinking of his earlier conversation with Tess. You
could tell she and Ellamae came from the same family
tree. Tess's flat responses couldn't have gotten any more
direct, though in a closemouthed way that left him more
frustrated than before. He sensed it wouldn't be the same
with Ellamae. But to get from her, you had to give. "As
for what happened, I got bored with things. And then I got
hurt."

"Yeah, we heard about it. That bull tossed you six ways
to Sunday, didn't he?"

He nodded.

"I saw you limping some when you got here. Noticed

it got worse after you stood at the grill a while. I thought that rehab place fixed you up."

He shrugged. "After a long day, I get to feeling some aches."

"Don't we all." She gave him a surprisingly sweet smile. "Well, you shoot pretty straight yourself, so I'll tell you this. Roselynn might come back here ready to chat with you, but she won't allow you much without a sugar coating on it. Tess won't allow you anything at all."

He nodded again.

"Found that out already, huh?"

"Yeah."

She smiled. "Then, it's lucky you got me. I'll flap my jaws in a good cause any day."

Together, they shot glances toward the doorway. All clear.

"Okay, then." Caleb tipped his chair forward another notch. "Start flapping."

TESS PUT THE CARAFE of hot chocolate in the center of the tray and surrounded it with coffee mugs. The girls didn't need the extra sugar this late, but since they wouldn't sleep much tonight, anyway, that didn't matter.

What mattered was what *she* needed, and that was to get rid of Caleb. To safeguard her peace of mind. Her sanity. And maybe to protect her heart. Something inside still hurt after that unfeeling apology he'd given her.

Roselynn came into the kitchen and set the pie plate on the counter near the sink. "Need any help?"

"No, I've got it, thanks."

She looked over at the carafe. "You have enough for Caleb to have a cup of chocolate, too, don't you?"

"Yes, Mom. But I would imagine he'll be leaving any minute now."

Leaving…as he'd done so long ago.

She tightened her grip on the handle of the carafe. How could that one word, that one thought, fill her with both bitterness and longing at the same time?

"I don't know," her mother said.

Tess started, afraid she had spoken her question aloud.

But Roselynn stood looking through the doorway. "It appears he and El have settled in for a nice little chat."

"Oh, have they?" Tess grabbed the tray. If there was one thing Aunt El was known for, it was believing she knew what was best for everyone—and not hesitating to tell them.

Tess didn't want to think about the earful Caleb might be getting. But she certainly wanted to put a stop to it. "Can you bring the napkins, please?"

"Tess…" Roselynn frowned.

"What's wrong, Mom? Headache?"

"No…nothing. I'll go get some more napkins from the pantry."

In the dining room again, Tess saw her mother had been right. Caleb and Ellamae had their heads closer together than two sticky buns in a breadbasket.

She sailed across the room and plunked the tray on the table between them. Caleb backed off just quickly enough to keep from getting hit in the head.

A head that was as hard as that bull's he'd been talking about earlier. She ought to know.

"Hot chocolate!" Nate yelled.

The girls dropped their cards and clustered around the smaller table. Tess kept busy pouring drinks and passing out not-quite-filled mugs. No sense inviting spills. Upholstery and rug cleaning were expensive.

She looked through the doorway of the room to the

grandfather clock in the hall. Almost nine. The girls would be up for hours yet, if they ever did get to bed.

She'd had to laugh. All those empty guest rooms upstairs, and they had chosen to sleep on the couches and floor in the living room.

"It's getting late," she told them. "Time to go off to the other room, now." At least that put them closer to their sleeping arrangements for the night.

"Come on in with us, Caleb," Nate said.

Tess could have won money on that being her daughter's next step. "No, Caleb's going to be leaving." Again, that word caught at her, made her want to sigh. Her voice shook just a bit as she added, "You girls go on."

Up went the stubborn jaw. Another step in her daughter's attempt to get her own way.

"But Mo-om," Nate wailed. So predictable. "He's drinking his hot chocolate, too."

"He can drink it here."

"Why can't he come with us?" Nate's bottom lip jutted out.

Tess gripped the edges of the tray. "Anastasia Lynn La-Salle," she said evenly.

Lissa poked Nate in the ribs. "C'mon, Nate. When it's all your names, you know you're in big trouble."

Before Nate could say another word that would get her in deeper, before Tess could add something she might regret, Caleb spoke up.

"You run off, now, like your mama says. I'll see you girls in the morning."

Tess turned to him. Bad enough her own daughter was trying to make the rules around here. She didn't need him attempting to call the shots, too. She didn't need him at all.

"I don't think so, Caleb," she said, her chin as high as

Nate's had been. "From now on, if we need to discuss any business at all, we'll meet at the office."

He smiled, took a sip of his chocolate, licked whipped cream from his top lip.

Tess set her jaw and glared at him.

"Fine by me," he replied.

She narrowed her eyes. She'd never known him to give in so easily.

"Business. Office. Got it." He smiled again and set the mug on his table. "But I will see the girls tomorrow morning, anyhow. At breakfast."

"What?"

He swept his arm out, gesturing at the space around them. "This *is* a bed-and-breakfast. I assume your mama serves breakfast to her guests. As I've just decided to take a room here for the rest of my stay in town, I reckon that qualifies me for the meals."

The girls broke into cheers loud enough to make the mugs on the tray rattle.

Or maybe that came from Tess's suddenly shaking hands. She clutched the tray, wishing she could hold it against her like a shield. She needed some kind of armor against Caleb—because obviously no one else in the room planned to help her.

The girls were too occupied in high-fiving Caleb and each other. Aunt El was too busy smirking over the turn of events she'd probably brought about herself. And her mother…

Her mother was standing there smiling quietly, eyes aglow at the idea of a paying guest.

Tess swallowed a sigh verging on a sob of despair.

Much as she wanted to kick Caleb out of their home, she knew full well her mom couldn't afford to turn away any source of income. And as she gazed into his shining green eyes, she realized he knew it, too.

Caleb had himself a room at the bed-and-breakfast for as long as he wanted it.

And Tess had hold of a time bomb with an ever-shortening fuse.

Chapter Five

As Tess crossed the downstairs entryway, the grandfather clock in the corner chimed.

Two in the morning.

Fighting back a yawn, she climbed the stairs to the second floor again. She'd known not to expect the girls to settle down any time soon, but her patience had deserted her. She'd decided a little friendly caution to the group couldn't hurt.

The warning *had* reduced their giggles enough that she could barely hear them from the top of the stairway.

Roselynn's bedroom lay at the far end of the hall. The noise from the living room wouldn't bother her. Still, the warning to the girls had been good training for them, for the days when they had paying guests at the inn.

If they ever did again.

In the hallway, she came to an abrupt halt.

They *did* have a guest on the premises.

After the hour of troubled sleep she'd just tossed and turned through, how could she have forgotten that? Especially when that brief nap had been filled with images of their new boarder?

As if she'd slipped back into those fitful dreams, the door to her right opened slowly. Silently. Caleb stood framed in the opening, the glow from the hall fixture highlighting him. She gulped, staring at his tousled dark hair and eyes hazy with sleep, to a bare chest dusted with dark hair that arrowed down toward the pair of blue cotton pajama bottoms riding low on his hips.

He stood so close, she would need only to take a step to touch him.

She gulped again, feeling a stirring inside that sent her hands grasping to close her robe. Grasping—and finding nothing but her long sleep T-shirt. It covered her completely. She'd had no reservations about going downstairs to the girls without her robe.

But, oh, did she have her doubts about that decision now.

Caleb stood looking at her as if the T-shirt were made of see-through nylon with only a few velvet swatches in strategic spots for decoration.

"I'm sorry," she said coolly, though she'd grown hot all over in response to his hungry gaze. She forced herself to put her hands calmly by her sides. "Did the girls wake you?"

He shook his head emphatically, as if trying to clear it. "No, you did, pounding up and down the stairs. Thought we were having an earthquake."

"Very funny."

He grinned, a sleepy, crooked smile that only cranked up the heat within her. "Didn't you feel the walls shake?"

She could feel herself shaking now, all right, to the point she had to fight her need to grab on to something solid.

Like Caleb.

"Sorry," she said again, abruptly this time. "I'll try to be quieter in future."

"Good." He slumped sideways, bracing one shoulder

against the door frame. "I can't imagine you'd keep your guests very long if you go around disturbing their sleep."

"Then they shouldn't disturb mine." *Oh, great.* She'd snapped the words without thinking, more in irritation at herself for her weakness than anything else. Maybe he wouldn't realize what she'd said. Maybe he would think she meant the girls downstairs.

But, even half-asleep, he caught on quickly. "Did I bother your dreams tonight, Tess?"

"No."

He reached out to brush her hair back from her cheek. His fingertips whisked across her skin, sending a tickle along her jaw. He leaned close. Closer. She fought the urge to tilt her head the slightest bit, to let him cup her cheek with his palm. To lean even closer in anticipation.

"You never were very good at lying," he murmured.

The combination of his softened voice and less-than-gentle words made her breath catch in surprise. As she backed a step away, his fingertips raised a trail of goose bumps on her skin. "I try not to."

"Good. Then, you'll probably want to take back what you said. I *did* bother your sleep, didn't I?"

She attempted indignation, but the sound that came from her throat could have passed for a yearning sigh. Why couldn't things have ended differently years ago?

She stiffened her shoulders and raised her chin. "The fact you feel you can ask that bothers me," she said, side-stepping one truth but forcing herself to go full steam ahead toward another. "There's no sense in your worrying about whether or not you affect my dreams. The sleeping ones, anyhow. You gave up that right a long time ago."

He raised his hand again.

Smiling grimly, she backed another step, edging out

of his reach. "I think you already know what you did to destroy my waking dreams. But that was a long time ago, too. We're beyond that and on to something new." Giving a firm nod, she added, "Breakfast will be served at eight. Then we'll take care of the business that brought you back to town. Meanwhile, have a good rest of the night."

She turned and walked away, blinking rapidly to hold back tears. Of frustration? Anger? Sadness? She couldn't tell.

She knew only that she'd been kidding herself when she'd thought about needing to hold on to something solid, like Caleb.

She'd felt the need, all right. To be close to him again. To relive the past with him. To revisit those days she had refused to talk about earlier when he'd brought them up to her.

Need had to give way to reality. Trying to make a relationship with Caleb into something solid, something lasting, would never work. The past had already shown her the truth. The real man didn't want her.

She'd just have to try harder to keep the dream-Caleb out of her bed.

No worries about that at the moment, unfortunately. This encounter with him guaranteed that in the hours until daybreak she'd find herself wide-awake and more restless than before. If a few minutes in the hallway had been that dangerous, what would happen if she spent all day tomorrow on the road with him?

She just wouldn't, that's all. She'd use her sleepless hours to revise tomorrow's schedule, making sure she and Caleb spent as little time alone together as possible until she could pull herself together....

On second thought, she'd better revamp her schedule for the week.

"ANOTHER SWEET ROLL, Caleb?" Roselynn held the wicker basket toward him. Earlier she'd made a point of saying how nice it was to have a man at the table with them again.

He'd never had the pleasure of starting the morning off with a houseful of women. He found it a dubious pleasure, at best.

The little girls chattered constantly, sounding like a bunch of jaybirds perched on a humming telephone wire.

Roselynn seemed distracted now. The few times she attempted conversation, all she did was ask him if he wanted more of anything. Maybe the kids were giving her a headache.

He couldn't complain about the breakfast. He *could* complain about his second hostess, Tess, who didn't seem to care whether he ate or not. Obviously, she still felt riled.

So did he, as a matter of fact. Riled.

And intrigued.

Roselynn waved the sweet rolls at him again. "Yes, ma'am," he said hastily, "I'd like another of those."

Before he could pluck one from the basket, Nate snatched the top one out from under his hand.

"Nate," Tess snapped. "That was rude."

The girl shrugged. "Sorry," she muttered.

"Don't tell me, tell your guest."

Nate gave him a wide smile. "Sorry, Caleb. You want to share this one with me?"

"No, thanks, I'll get my own."

"Let me get some fresh from the oven," Roselynn said, reaching for the basket. She rushed off as though she couldn't wait to escape the tension between Tess and Nate.

He looked over at Tess, all prim and proper with a long-sleeved shirt buttoned up to her chin. A far cry from her outfit of the previous night. That loose, flowing T-shirt she'd worn hanging down to her knees hadn't given anything away. But his imagination didn't need a handout. He could envision what lay beneath the T-shirt just as easily as he could see how uncomfortable she still felt about getting caught in it.

All through breakfast, she'd refused to make eye contact with him. Her gaze kept moving to her briefcase on the chair in the corner. She wanted his business taken care of. She wanted him gone. He'd picked up on her feeling during supper the night before, and that—and sheer stubbornness—had only added to his list of reasons for taking the room at the inn.

Could he blame her for wanting to get rid of him? Maybe not. But he couldn't give her the satisfaction of leaving. He'd tried to explain to her what had happened years ago. She'd made it more than plain she didn't want to discuss it. Their past was in the past. She'd said it herself.

Looking down, he stabbed at the ham steak on his plate.

He still had his future to take care of.

She seemed equally certain of the need to make sure he didn't have a future around here.

After their standoff upstairs in the hall last night, he couldn't say she had things wrong. Staying this close to her might bring more trouble than he wanted to handle. He'd touched her face. Hadn't wanted to stop touching her. But she'd backed away as if he'd been a rattler with his tail rising. It had taken him a hell of an effort to let her walk off.

Another few minutes and he might've done something to get his face smacked. As if her verbal slap about her dreams hadn't made him feel bad enough.

You gave up that right a long time ago.

Maybe one of these days he'd find out what rights he

did have with her. Now that could get interesting, at least for as long as he stayed in town. Money wasn't his only means of making an impression. He swallowed a grin along with another mouthful of coffee.

"Mom," Nate blurted, distracting him. "I forgot. When we went to the store yesterday, Mr. Harley said to say howdy."

"Oh, did he?"

He looked over at Tess. She'd sounded a little put out about the announcement. Asking her directly wouldn't get him anywhere. "I remember a Harley from school." Harley wouldn't remember him, though. The kid in his homeroom was too rich for the likes of him. "Doesn't his daddy own the general store?"

"He did," Tess said. "Joe has it now."

"Does he?" He smiled at Nate.

"Yep." She nodded. "And he makes money, hand over fist."

"Nate." Tess's voice had sharpened.

"Well, that's what Aunt El says. Right, Gram?"

Roselynn had just returned to the room and set the basketful of sweet rolls next to his plate.

Not waiting for an answer, Nate leaned closer to him. "Mr. Harley has the biggest store in Flagman's Folly. And he wants to marry Mom."

"Nate!" This time, Tess's voice could've cut the slice of ham steak sitting on his plate. "I think it's time for you and the girls to go and straighten up the living room."

Her friends promptly put their utensils down and began to rise.

Nate remained seated. "Why? There's nobody here but Caleb. He doesn't mind."

"Anastasia Lynn."

The girl rolled her eyes. "Oka-*ay*. Come on, Caleb, you can help me move the couch back."

Slowly, he released the death grip he'd held on his knife and fork.

"We'll take care of that later," Tess told her. "Caleb's still eating his breakfast. You go along, now."

The other girls pushed in their chairs.

Nate pushed out her bottom lip.

That had him biting back a comment. No doubt about it, Tess had her work cut out with this little one. But it wasn't his place to say anything.

Nate finally got up and shoved her chair up to the table. The kid had a lot of energy.

"See you later," she said to him.

He nodded. When she'd left the room, he turned back to Tess. Better to think about teasing her—and not about some guy who wanted her for his bride. "Paybacks," he murmured.

"What?"

"When you're a real handful as a kid, don't folks say to watch out, because 'you'll grow up to have kids of your own someday'?"

"No."

Roselynn laughed. "Oh, yes, they do, sugar. And he has a point." She turned to him. "Tess was an outright handful herself, you know."

"Mo-om," Tess protested, her tone sounding exactly like Nate's. "Let's not get into—" At the sound of footsteps in the kitchen, she stopped.

A real shame. He'd looked forward to hearing a few stories.

Ellamae ambled into the room as if she owned the place. She carried a coffee mug that matched those on the table. "Am I in time for breakfast?"

"Sweet rolls right out of the oven," he said, moving the basket to a space in front of an empty seat.

"That'll do for starters." Ellamae plopped into the chair and took a roll. "And just how is everyone this fine morning?"

"Lovely," Roselynn said. "We were just talking about Tess."

"Who is just getting ready to go to work," Tess said. "Speaking of which, aren't you on your way to Town Hall now, Aunt El? Is the Double S closed today?"

He almost smiled at her innocent tone.

"Oh, it's open." Ellamae turned to him. "Normally, I pick up an order to go and bring it over to the courtroom. But I felt a need to speak to my sister this morning."

"Perfect timing," Tess said. "Caleb and I are just leaving. Aren't we, Caleb?"

"Without brushing our teeth?" he asked, his tone as deliberately innocent as hers had been. "Does Nate get away with that?"

Her expression could have made a bull run for cover.

"*After* we brush, of course." She stood and pushed her chair beneath the table.

"Ah. Then we *are* just leaving," he said, following her lead.

"We'll see you at supper then, Caleb," Roselynn said.

"I'll be here," he confirmed.

He left the dining room at Tess's heels.

Much as he liked the thought of watching her squirm while her mama and aunt told tales on her, he'd come up with another idea he liked much better.

Getting her alone.

HER SISTER, Roselynn, made a sweet roll you could really sink your teeth into. Ellamae surveyed the breakfast table with satisfaction. But before she had eaten more than two rolls and a side of bacon, Nate and the girls came back into the dining room like a swarm of honeybees headed for the hive.

She held back a chuckle. If she'd guessed right by the look on Caleb's face, before too much time had passed, he intended to do a bit of swarming of his own—over Tess.

"Where's Caleb?" Nate demanded, looking wildly around the room as if he'd hidden beneath one of the tables.

"He and your mama left just a few minutes ago," Roselynn said.

"Rats." Nate slumped in obvious disappointment.

"What's the trouble?" Ellamae asked. "He'll be back tonight."

"That's too late. We have to find him." Nate sidestepped closer to the two women. Her friends crowded in behind her. "We got a *great* idea," she announced.

Ellamae couldn't wait. "And what might that be?"

"We gotta get Caleb to stay in Flagman's Folly."

"But why, sugar?"

"Oh, Gram," Nate said, as if it were obvious. "This town is soooo boring. We need *something* to make it special. And Caleb's famous."

"He's a rodeo star," her friend Lissa added.

"Ex," Ellamae said flatly, but as she'd expected, no one paid any attention to that.

"So we got an idea to get him to stay." Nate put her hands on her hips and beamed at them. "We get him to marry Mom."

Roselynn choked on a mouthful of tea.

With one hand, Ellamae patted her back. With the other, she swiped another sweet roll. A conversation like this one called for extra sustenance. "And just how did y'all happen to come by that thought?"

"Easy," Nate said.

"She doesn't want her mom to marry Mr. Harley," Lissa put in.

"Caleb's richer," Nate said.

"And cuter," added Lissa.

"And *a star*," chorused the two remaining girls.

"Oh, sugar, I don't know—"

"Well," Ellamae broke in, "it's an idea, all right, Nate. But you and the girls better just forget about that for now. Let your mama and Caleb have some time together, see what happens. You never know. Everything might just come to pass the way you want it, without your helping things along."

"You like the idea, though, right, Aunt El? Right, Gram?" In her eagerness, Nate leaned so far forward she almost fell into the basket of sweet rolls. "You want Caleb to stay here, too, don't ya?"

"It has its possibilities, I'll admit," Ellamae told her. "But as I said, let's give it some time. You girls go on about your business. Unless you want to help clear the dishes."

"No, thanks." Nate backed up, almost trampling her friends. "We already have to fix the living room. Come on, guys."

All four girls turned and fled.

Ellamae laughed.

Roselynn smiled, shaking her head gently. "Those kids. What a wild idea."

Abruptly, Ellamae stopped laughing. "What's so wild about it?"

"For a rich man like Caleb? He has a ranch and a big

house up in Montana. Why in the world would he want to move back to a little place like Flagman's Folly?"

"Two reasons." Ellamae held up a finger still sticky with icing. "One reason went out the door with him earlier." Another finger. "And the other just ran into the next room with her friends."

Roselynn stared at her. "Oh, no. That's not a reason. Not for Caleb. He doesn't know."

"He could find out."

Now Roselynn shook her head in earnest. "Not from us, he can't. Our lives wouldn't be worth the price of a three-day-old loaf of bread if Tess ever found out. Besides, *she* doesn't even realize that *we* know."

"Then I guess the girls are right."

"About what?"

"He's got to come around to the idea of marrying Tess."

Her sister gasped. "What makes you think she'd want to marry him now, after he already left her once and broke her heart? You remember how she moped around here."

"I do. But I also see how she's been acting since he's come back again. Like a firecracker ready to explode."

"She doesn't want to get hurt again."

"Of course not. And she's got her defenses up high against that, all right. Caleb's gonna have a time knocking them down. But you called it, too. He won't just up and decide on marriage all on his own. I imagine he'll need to be roped and hog-tied by his friends."

Roselynn set her teacup so firmly into its saucer, Ellamae felt sure it had cracked. "Those are children you're talking about, El. You are *not* going to get them involved in something like—"

"Settle down, settle down," she said, waving her hands to calm Rose. One of her hands just happened to pass over the basket, so she snagged another sweet roll. "I don't plan for those girls to do anything about it at all. This situation calls for a couple of mature, educated people to handle it."

"Like who?" Roselynn demanded.

"Like us, of course."

Her sister sighed. "Oh, Ellamae, it's so obvious our Nate's related to you. You both do come up with the wildest ideas." Grabbing a sweet roll, she smiled. "You always *were* good that way." She rested her elbows on the table and leaned forward. "So, what've you got in mind?"

Chapter Six

The sun had crawled well above the horizon by the time they finally left the bed-and-breakfast. A hot morning already, even for the start of June.

Caleb smiled to himself. Tess would soon regret that buttoned-up shirt she'd worn today.

She moved toward the parking area at a near-trot. He kept to a slower pace, but a steady one, eager for the chance to be alone with her. That spark he couldn't have missed between them last night had him curious. Had she felt it, too?

Then he recalled Nate's statement about the local store owner—the one who made money "hand over fist." She'd seemed impressed by that. What about Tess? What would she think when she found out how easily *he* could give the man a run for his money?

"So," he asked, "what Nate said at the table. You planning on marrying Harley?"

His question put a definite hitch in her stride. He smiled.

Without turning, she said coolly, "I haven't decided yet."

"Sounds like he could take care of you in style. According to Nate and your aunt Ellamae, that is."

"Yes."

Yes, *what?* He knew she and Roselynn were struggling. The man's financial status had to mean something to her. She stopped and faced him. His heart revved up with the crazy thought he'd just given her reason to decide in Harley's favor.

A frown line creased her forehead. "What was that my mother said about seeing you at supper?"

His heart settled back into its normal rhythm. Her mind hadn't been on Harley at all. "We renegotiated my reservation while you were in talking with the girls this morning. I'm paying a little extra and getting another meal. On top of the *other* perks," he said, grinning.

The glint in her eyes told him she'd understood his teasing. Her suddenly expressionless face let him know how little she liked the idea of sharing another meal with him at the inn every day.

"Well," she snapped, "since you've made arrangements of your own already, you won't mind that I've had a change to my plans, too. I've got some errands to run. I'm sure you'll be able to amuse yourself until supper tonight."

Now, *that* bothered him. He'd hired her to find him a ranch. "What do you mean, you've got errands? I thought you were all mine today." Despite his annoyance, it gave him satisfaction to see the soft pink blush filling her face. It also offered him a sliver of hope as sweet as Ellamae's pecan pie.

He thought back again to their meeting in the hallway last night. The look in her eyes then, the expression on her face when he'd touched her—they meant something. What, he didn't know, but he had a feeling it would be in his best interest to find out.

Besides, she'd said it herself, she hadn't yet promised herself to that Harley character.

"Actually," she said, "it may surprise you to hear this, but you're not the only item on my agenda. I've got business to take care of. First, I need to stop by the office to pick up some business cards and brochures."

He raised his brows. "You're planning on advertising to the critters out in the wild?"

"Very funny. No. Dana and I are doing an advertising blitz to try to…to increase our client list. I'm going to hit all the businesses on Signal Street today."

She turned and walked away, as if that ended their conversation. A few spaces short of his pickup truck, she stopped beside the old Toyota he'd seen yesterday.

If she thought she could shake him off with a trumped-up list of errands, she'd have to think again. Besides, her plans fit nicely into his own agenda. He would have had as much chance to flash his cash out in the desert as she'd have had passing out brochures. Now he could make like a rodeo star the length of Signal Street—with Tess right there to see him shine.

He moved to the passenger side of the Toyota and looked at her over the roof. "No problem. I'll go with you. Get a chance to say hello to folks I haven't seen in a while."

Her face fell, but she nodded shortly.

The cramped front seat wouldn't allow much room for him to stretch out his legs or ease his bad knee. Before he could suggest taking the truck, Tess had slipped inside and cranked the engine. He shrugged, then shoehorned himself into the car, sure he'd eventually wish he hadn't.

On the other hand, their close quarters kept her well within reaching distance. He recalled the warmth of her cheek against his fingertips the night before. This arrangement could work in his favor.

She looked away, carefully checking her mirrors before backing out of the parking space.

After they'd gone a block in silence, he decided playing along with her would work, too. "Good idea about the promo," he said easily. "You ought to work up some for the bed-and-breakfast. Your mama needs to get going if she wants any takers for those empty rooms upstairs."

She pulled over to the curb and jammed on the brakes so abruptly, his knee hit the dashboard. Pain radiated down to his ankle. He swore under his breath and made a big production of putting on his seat belt. She ignored that.

"Caleb, what exactly are you up to?" she demanded. "Why are you so interested in the inn?"

"I'm not int—"

She ran right over him. "And how is it you oh-so-conveniently had your suitcase in your truck last night? What happened to your plans to stay out of town? You had everything 'covered'—or so you'd said."

"This works out better." The idea of her seeing him throw money around town had started to appeal to him more than he'd thought.

"For *you,* maybe."

Yeah, his decision to take the room at the bed-and-breakfast had riled her. Not a good thing, maybe, in view of his plans. Even knowing it would make her more irritated, he couldn't help laughing at her response.

She exhaled forcefully. "Don't you have a reservation somewhere?"

"There's not a hotel, motel or town, for that matter, within fifty miles of Flagman's Folly, as you—being in the business of selling property and all—must surely know."

"All right, knock off the sarcasm." She pulled back onto the street and continued driving.

He shook his head. "Better watch yourself. I'm sure it wouldn't sit right with Dana to hear how her 'glorified file clerk', as you called yourself, is treating her biggest client."

She gave a snort equal to one of her aunt Ellamae's. "You mean 'the client with the biggest head,' don't you?" she asked sweetly.

"Maybe some people around here don't think so."

"You can't trust the judgment of *some people*. Especially when they're under the age of ten."

She'd noticed Nate and company's hero worship of him, too, then. She didn't need to sound so sour about it. "It's not like I'd asked for the attention."

"Of course not."

And she'd accused *him* of sarcasm.

She probably thought he'd encouraged the kids.

"Hey, it comes with the territory." When she didn't respond, he continued mildly, "We seem to have strayed from the subject of your mama. I was only asking about promo out of concern for her."

"Why would you even care?"

He looked at her without speaking, and this time her face flushed twice as fast. She grasped the steering wheel more tightly and swallowed hard before replying. "Never mind. But I'm sure she's working on some advertising for the inn."

"Not by the sound of it last night. Said it costs money."

"Which we don't have," she said flatly. "Is that what you're getting at?"

He raised his hands in mock surrender. "Whoa, now. I'm not getting at anything, only repeating what I'd heard from her. You know, I could give—"

"No." She stopped at a traffic light and stared straight ahead, her hands now in a white-knuckled grip on the wheel. "I know Mom's happy to have a paying guest, but that's as far as your money goes. I also know you're rich.

Richer than anyone here in Flagman's Folly—probably everyone put together. But we don't need your charity."

"Where'd you get that idea?" he asked, trying to keep it low-key. "I was only going to say I could give my promo people a call and see if they could recommend some ideas for your mama."

"Oh."

"Yeah, *oh*," he echoed, losing the effort to hold himself in check. "What do you know about charity, anyway?" he demanded. "I was at the receiving end of more handouts than you'll ever see in your life."

The light changed. The car jerked forward. Now he took a turn staring through the windshield. But he couldn't seem to shut up. "Your family *never* needed anything from me, did they? Never wanted it, either."

"You didn't meet my family."

"Not true."

"My mother never told me." It sounded like an accusation.

"She wouldn't know. It wasn't your mama I came across, anyhow, but your granddaddy."

She gasped. "You spoke with my grandfather? About what?"

He heard the edginess in her tone. Even after all these years, the idea that he'd talked to the man upset her that much? "I asked to do some work around your property. Yank weeds, cut grass. He just stood there in the doorway of that big old house and informed me he had 'no need to hire someone from the street.'"

She pulled the Toyota over to the curb in front of her office and threw the gearshift into Park. "You came to my house? Even after I'd asked you not to?"

Her voice shook, with rage or fear, he didn't know. But he could tell she hadn't gotten his meaning, maybe hadn't even taken in the words he'd said. She'd focused on what worried her most.

"No," he replied, as softly as he could. "That was before we were together."

"Oh," she said again. She ran her hands along the steering wheel. "Putting my foot in my mouth twice in one conversation, that's a record for me."

"It happens when people make assumptions."

"I'm sorry, Caleb." She looked away. "I…I'll be right back."

She'd opened the door and was out of the car before he'd taken his seat belt off.

All this, because he'd offered to help her mama. Would she have reacted as strongly if Harley had made the suggestion? Did she have a long history with the man, too? The questions left a bitter taste in his mouth.

He shouldn't care about her relationships with other men. About her anger. Or her apology. Or what she thought about him.

He shouldn't care about her at all.

Yet he did.

She hurried away from the Toyota, leaving him cooling his heels—but that's about as far as it went. His thoughts about her continued to keep the rest of him heated. The questions he'd obsessed over since the night before wouldn't leave him alone.

She crossed the sidewalk to her office, her dark curls gleaming in the sun. That pink shirt and her snug jeans sent his thoughts into a gallop. His memory, too. Once upon a time, he'd committed every inch of her to that memory. Did she ever think about that time, too? Maybe getting caught in her pajamas last night wasn't the only reason she'd covered up almost to her chin today.

He shoved open the door and climbed from the car. As

he straightened his left knee, pain arced through it, making him grit his teeth. That knock into the dashboard had set any progress he'd made back a notch.

He leaned against the Toyota and recalled, once again, the scene outside his bedroom door last night. The thought sparked yet more memories. Was the rest of her still as soft as he recalled? Still the same shade of peach all over?

He wiped his brow, suddenly as sweaty as if he'd spent the morning sunbathing on a beach.

Yeah, she'd gotten him heated—in mind and body both.

That knowledge, and the fact he couldn't turn the feelings off, disgusted him. Just as he'd once disgusted her granddaddy.

The man had said a lot more to him that day, made comments he would never tell Tess. Or anyone. Comments about "streetwalkers" and "white trash" and "people who ought to stay where they belong."

That memory made him hot all over, this time with shame. A shame he'd sworn he'd never let himself feel again.

Years ago, those times he and Tess spent together, she had left her house to meet him. She had slept with him. But she'd never taken him to meet her family. Never wanted to bring him around her friends. He didn't have to ask why.

He wasn't good enough for them.

He wasn't good enough for anyone in Flagman's Folly.

Yeah, well, that had changed. As she had said, he'd gotten rich. He'd make sure she knew just how much he was worth now. And he'd make damn sure *everyone* in town knew it, too.

Chapter Seven

A short while later, when the door of Wright Place Realty opened, Caleb forced his expression into neutral.

But it wasn't Tess leaving the office. Instead, a tall, dark-haired man stepped out and closed the door behind him. Too tall for Joe Harley.

What business did this guy have with Tess?

He shook his head at his own resentful thought. Real estate business, of course. What else? And what was it to him? Nothing. Same as Nate's claim that Harley wanted to marry her mama. He'd better remember that.

Hell, he'd do even better getting a handle on this sudden streak of jealousy he didn't know he had.

To his surprise, the man walked toward him, grinning, with his hand outstretched.

"Hey, Caleb. Long time, no see."

At the last second, Caleb recognized him. "Ben." Ben Sawyer, one of his former classmates. It gave him satisfaction to see he could look the other man eye to eye now. All through school, he'd been a head shorter than Ben.

Though they were the same age, he'd wound up graduating high school a year behind the lot of them. Ben. Paul Wright, Dana's husband. Sam Robertson and a slew of others. He'd rather not think about the reasons for that.

"Yeah," he said, "it's been a long time. I'm a stranger to Flagman's Folly now."

"Are you kidding?" Ben laughed. "Around here, you're considered the most well-known person in the Southwest."

He smiled grimly. "Guess the media covered my downfall thoroughly enough." Not exactly the image he wanted to portray.

"I wasn't talking about your downfall, more like your local-boy-does-good career."

"The rodeo-crazy kids in this town." He knew it.

"Not just them. Everyone in the county followed your time on the circuit. But yeah, those kids really took an interest. You're their hero." The other man hesitated, then added, "You'll get back to riding again soon?"

He shook his head. "Not soon. Not ever."

Ben exhaled heavily. "That's tough."

Next, he would mumble something and make an uncomfortable exit, the way everyone else who'd known Caleb before the accident did. Not wanting to see that, he asked, "What are you doing in town, instead of working your ranch?" He looked over at Tess's office. "You thinking of buying some property?"

"No." Now Ben seemed uncomfortable. He turned, gesturing to the storefront. "I own the building. I hear you're looking for some land in the area, though."

"Tess told you?" What else had she said about him? Then again, considering the fear she still seemed to have that folks would find out about their past, she probably hadn't said anything much other than that.

"Not Tess. I had to make a stop at Town Hall yesterday afternoon and heard the news there."

Caleb raised an eyebrow. He knew what that meant. "Let me guess. Ellamae filled you in."

"Ellamae did," Ben confirmed.

Odd. His return to town would've made the rounds instantly, of course. No getting away from that. But how had she known so early on about his plan to invest in property? Had Tess talked about him to her aunt, at least?

"Anyhow," Ben was saying, "you won't go wrong buying land here. And we all figured it was only a matter of time before you'd come back to your roots." He nodded as if to emphasize his words. "I'll see you around town."

Caleb watched the other man walk away, his stride steady and certain, strong evidence that Ben Sawyer felt he owned more than just the building in front of him. He owned a place in his hometown.

Not something Caleb could claim.

As for those roots Ben had mentioned…

He took a seat on a bench near the real estate office and stretched his good leg full length. The twinge in his bad leg told him not to risk it.

Back when he'd lived here, he wouldn't have called what he'd had "roots." More like a rolling mass of tumbleweed, with no ties and no reason for them. No attention from anyone. Positive attention, anyway. Except for Dori and Manny from the Double S. Ellamae, at times. And Tess. Or so he'd thought…

He shied away from going down that road. Better to focus on Ben.

Ben, who had just spoken as if he felt Caleb was a part of Flagman's Folly. And as if the townsfolk might think the same. Did the man mean they believed that now, based on Caleb's success in rodeo? Or could he really have meant folks felt Caleb belonged even when he'd lived here? Folks not like Tess's granddaddy?

He shook his head at the confusion the questions had brought on.

The door of the office opened again, and this time

Tess did emerge from the building. She went over to the Toyota and dropped a package onto the backseat. Then she squared her shoulders and turned toward him, her mouth set in a smile.

Maybe Dana had given her a talking-to in the office. And maybe Tess had accepted that she had to follow through on her duties—whether she liked the idea or not.

"Let's go," she said.

He didn't much like her clipped tones. She'd sounded almost like her granddaddy. Instead of rising, he patted the wooden seat beside him. "Take a break."

Her gaze shot to his left knee and away again. She probably thought he needed a rest. She opened her mouth to say something pitying. He could see it in her eyes. But then she closed her mouth without uttering a word.

Two people in a row who hadn't voiced their sympathy. He ought to be grateful for that. He didn't need pity from them. From anyone.

He didn't need to bow down to them anymore, either. "Don't worry, that crack against the dashboard didn't do much damage. I'll be able to walk again." An ironic thing for him to say, considering the doctors had once held it in doubt. But she didn't need to know that.

Her cheeks red, Tess moved over to the bench and sat, cautiously, as if expecting the wooden slats to give way beneath her. She looked tense as a first-time bull rider.

Though the sarcasm had felt justified, he'd have to stop. Now. He needed to get her loosened up a little, more receptive to him again. A losing battle, maybe, considering their history. But he wouldn't know unless he tried. Besides, he needed to get more in touch with what had gone on in Flagman's Folly since he'd left.

"Saw Ben Sawyer when he came out of your office," he said easily.

Her shoulders lowered a notch. "Did you?"

"Yeah. It took me a second to recognize him."

"Really? He hasn't changed a lot since high school."

He shrugged. "I didn't see much of him back then. I wasn't in any of the clubs or on any of the committees."

"Neither was I, except when they desperately needed extra help and Dana dragged me along." She looked straight ahead. With one hand, she brushed at her jeans. Trying to sweep away memories?

Would she have any better luck at that than he had?

"Yeah, Dana and Paul and Ben, they had a hand in everything. You and I weren't joiners," he said, feeling his way.

He wouldn't have made it onto the debate team, as Ben had. He'd never had a gift for quick answers. If he had, he might not have gotten knocked around so much by some of his mama's friends.

"Maybe," he ventured, "if we'd gotten tied up with more clubs at school or kept busier with friends, we might never have gotten together at all."

"Maybe not." Her voice sounded brittle, and she rushed on, "But Ben sure kept up with everything. They voted him onto the school council every year and made him president of both the junior and senior classes."

"I remember that. Always Mr. Personality, wasn't he?"

She nodded. "He still is. He's on the town council now."

"He told me he's your landlord."

She exhaled heavily, as if she'd been holding her breath, and curled her fingers into a loose fist on her knee. "Not mine. Dana's." Her tone had lost the brittleness, had become soft and low.

A car drove past on Signal Street, and he leaned closer, straining to hear her.

"Ben bought the building from the original owner. She rents the office from him."

"She? What about Paul? Doesn't he own half the business?"

Her shoulders stiffened again. "Paul—" Her voice broke. She cleared her throat and started again. "Paul isn't with us anymore."

Her reactions told him the man had done more than just leave town. He covered her hand with his. "What happened?"

"He was in the army and…he was killed overseas, a little over a year ago."

He shook his head in disbelief. When he could catch his breath, he asked quietly, "Dana's on her own now?"

Her eyes glittered suddenly. She looked away. "She has three children. Nate's friend Lissa is the oldest of them." She rose from the bench, her hand sliding free from his. "We ought to be going."

She said it as if she hadn't just dropped that news on him. Or as if she wanted an excuse to move away.

By the time he reached the car, she had slipped into the driver's seat and shut the door. He entered with less speed, trying to avoid hitting his knee. Attempting to recover from the shock of her words.

He felt no anger bubbling inside him now, just a churning mass of confusion. It left him uncertain of what to think. About anything.

In just a couple of conversations, his memories had been thrown offtrack, as unexpectedly as he'd been thrown off the last bull he'd ridden. And with just as many life-changing effects.

Paul…gone.

Ben…assuming Caleb would come home again.

The townsfolk…believing that he belonged.

It was a lot for him to take in at once.

Could he have gotten things wrong, at least as far as some folks were concerned? Did it matter? He still had more than enough reason to show the rest of them just what he'd become.

His cell phone vibrated. He pulled it from his pocket. Seeing the name and number on the screen gave him pause.

"I'll leave you alone," Tess murmured, getting out of the car and closing the door softly behind her.

He eyed the phone again and then greeted his foreman, who had a list of questions for him. Fortunately, he had answers. Yet by the time he'd ended the call, he wondered just how much longer he could leave the man on his own to manage the ranch.

He glanced at Tess. She was leaning against the front fender of the car.

She had as good as given him an ultimatum for today.

Ben Sawyer had given him things to think about that might affect his strategy.

He raised the phone in the air, indicating he'd finished his call. When she entered the car again, he turned to her. "I may have to leave town sooner than I intended." Her chest rose with her indrawn breath. Some might have mistaken it for disappointment. He knew better. "Looks like we're in for another change to our schedules. Now, how about showing me some real estate."

THREE DAYS LATER, he'd not gotten an inch closer to his goal. Caleb's jaw felt so tight he wondered how he could swallow his morning coffee.

"May I be excused?" Nate asked.

That was a first.

Even Tess looked astounded by the girl's politeness. She

nodded as if afraid saying something to her might break the spell.

Nate got up and pushed her chair in to the table. "Can I go with you and Caleb today?"

Ah. That explained the sudden show of manners. Wouldn't last long. He knew without a doubt what Tess's answer would be.

"No, I'm afraid not," she said. "You'll be too busy, anyway. Gram tells me you've slacked off on your chores around here."

"I don't want to do chores." Her intentions thwarted now, she'd turned ornery as an irritated bull.

"Neither do the rest of us. But we do them, anyway."

"Well, I'm not going to. I'm tired of chores. And it's summertime." Her chin came up and her dark eyes flashed.

Caleb bit down on the words he wanted to say. He didn't have any right to say them. But he wished for once he could take on some of Tess's burden. Take away some of the tension between her and Nate.

"That's enough," Tess snapped. "You have no other big plans for today. You're doing your chores. Besides," she added brightly, "there's no better time than a Friday morning to check everything off your list so you'll have a fresh start for the weekend."

Tess really took that "checking off" business to heart. She had driven him from one distant ranch to another this week, none of which came close to what he'd told her he wanted. It seemed any property at all would do for her, so long as she could check *him* off her list—and get a fresh start on her life.

Nate managed to hold her tongue but turned abruptly and ran from the room.

Despite his irritation at Tess, the despairing look on her

face stunned him. He grabbed his empty mug and took a long swig of nonexistent coffee just to keep from reaching for her instead.

Chapter Eight

"Give me a minute," Tess told Caleb. "I want to run up and see Nate before we leave."

"I'll be outside."

As if she needed the reminder. She hadn't made a move without him in days. At this point, she wasn't sure just how much more of his company she could take.

He'd seemed edgy and irritable during their long drives. She'd made a list of the most far-flung properties she could find, but he'd asked her about locating something nearer to Flagman's Folly—exactly what she *didn't* want to do.

She walked past his bedroom and tried not to think of how he'd looked that night she'd met him at his doorway. How he'd touched her and what she had felt. More stress piled onto what she already had to deal with.

Every day, no matter how she tried to avoid it, their trips brought them closer to the town limits. Every day, her tension increased and her guilt grew. Thoughts ran continually through her head of Mom and Nate, Dana and her kids, and all they had to lose if she didn't earn this commission.

And none of that even came close to the most dangerous aspect of this whole disaster.

Caleb's story of meeting her grandfather had surprised her. But after jumping to conclusions with him that day, she didn't ask anything more. She didn't want to know. From then on, she'd stayed vigilant about watching what she said. Unfortunately, she didn't have that power over her thoughts.

Who was she kidding? She didn't have *any* control of her thoughts or emotions when she was with Caleb.

She pushed against Nate's door and lost her breath as she found herself looking straight at him.

At her daughter's insistence, the bedroom had been decorated in a cowboy theme, which she'd added to by covering the walls with rodeo souvenirs. From the poster beside the dresser, a larger-than-life-size Caleb Cantrell, Champion Bull Rider, stood staring back at Tess.

She had to force herself to drag her gaze away.

Nate lay sprawled on her bed surrounded by her collection of miniature horses.

"You okay?" Tess asked.

"Yeah." She didn't look up.

"Do you want to tell me what's bothering you? I know you don't like doing your chores, but you don't normally refuse like that."

"Nothing's bothering me."

"Oh. Well, then, I'll say goodbye. We're getting ready to go out to look at more property."

"Yeah, you said that. At breakfast. You're *always* leaving."

Tess looked at her in surprise. Was that what Nate's tantrum had been about? Missing her mother? "I know. But it's business."

"Yeah, and it's *always* business. Why can't you go by yourself for once? Why can't Caleb stay here with me and Gram and the guys?" She sat up on the bed and bounded to her feet, scattering toy horses over the floor. "Why do you *always* have to take him away?"

Before Tess could recover, Nate ran through the door.

Her knees shaking, Tess sank to the edge of the bed.

Suddenly she felt thankful for the trip out of town. She would deal with her emotions around Caleb now, including the guilt that had begun to plague her almost daily. She'd have to. Anything would be better than letting him stay here and spend any more time with Nate.

CALEB HAD MOVED outside to lean up against the Toyota. He'd gotten tired of waiting in the kitchen.

He was impatient—for yet another day of self-imposed torture, of spending hours alone with Tess while keeping his hands off her. Evenings were better, since he'd taken it upon himself to fix up Roselynn's decrepit shed in the backyard of the inn.

But the days alone with Tess... If he didn't get a break from the days, the unfulfilled lust might just break *him*.

Still, those long rides with her along empty desert roads between available properties had left him plenty of time for thinking.

He had to keep his head around her. He couldn't start anything that might keep him tied down. That wasn't part of his plan. His life was in Montana now. He had a ranch to run, people dependent upon him, a foreman who might go rogue any minute. He had too much happening outside this town. And too many bad memories of it to stay here.

Permanently, anyhow. For the short term, that was a different story, one he'd told himself all those long months in rehab.

His life in Montana—or anywhere—would never mean a thing until he'd done what he'd set out to do right here. He damn sure wouldn't give that up for a roll in the hay.

Not even with Tess.

She came out of the house, and he caught another look

at the bright, flower-printed shirt she'd picked to wear today. The shirt that made him think of hot nights in a garden and even hotter sex on the grass under the stars.

He slid into the Toyota and slammed the door behind him. He'd almost gotten himself pulled together by the time she buckled herself into the driver's seat.

"We're heading southeast today," she announced. "Going to look at a couple of places down near Carlsbad."

Grinding his teeth, he stared out through the windshield. Here he was, lusting after the woman no matter how much he tried to talk himself out of it, while she did her best to get rid of him. He'd asked her to find some property closer to town. Did she think he didn't know Carlsbad was about as far as they could go and still be in the same state?

"I think we'll skip the long trek today," he said.

She frowned.

Roselynn came out onto the back porch with a basket of laundry to hang on the line. Seeing them, she set the basket on the top step and crossed over to the car. "Since you're still here, I thought I'd ask if you'd like me to fix you up a picnic lunch or anything."

"No, thanks," he said. "I think the only trip we'll be taking today is down to Signal Street."

Her eyes lit up. "Nice to hear you'll be in town." She turned away and went right back past the laundry basket and into the house.

Shrugging, he turned to Tess. "We've got some unfinished business to take care of."

There she went with that white-knuckled choke hold on the steering wheel he'd seen the other day. It reminded him of himself as a kid, the first time he'd climbed onto the back of a mechanical bucking bronco and held on for dear life. It bothered him to think he gave her that same feeling of desperation.

It irritated the hell out of him that she didn't share his feelings of lust.

He forced a smile. "You never gave out that promo you have," he reminded her.

"Speaking of promo," she said tightly, "I see you've given Nate some of yours."

He nodded. "Yeah. I contacted my PR people, and they sent me some info to pass along to your mama. They threw in some of my stuff, too. Nate was there when we opened the package. So I gave her a poster. See?" He grinned. "I told you there was value in advertising. Now, handing your promo out today can do double duty. You never got around to showing me the sights in town, either."

Her fingers had loosened considerably on the steering wheel, but at his last words her expression turned downright suspicious. "Why is that important?"

What should he tell her?

Not the truth, that's for sure.

He planned to fling money around Flagman's Folly in a way that would make her and everyone else sit up and take notice—and then bow down and beg for more.

No, he couldn't tell her that. Instead, as always, he read his audience and came up with a good story.

"If I buy a sizable ranch, I'm going to need a good number of cowhands and someone to run it. I'd like to know what's available for them if they ever come this way. And for me, too, when I'm around."

Again, her mouth opened and shut again. No suspicion in her eyes now. Only a look of complete dismay.

Obviously, the thought that he would return to check on his property from time to time hadn't occurred to her.

And now that he'd brought it up, she didn't like the idea one bit.

But she would keep quiet about that. He'd bet on it.

Sure enough, when he didn't say anything else, she nodded.

"Yes, I guess you're right," she said finally. Grudgingly. She started the car and proceeded to Signal Street without saying another word.

He'd called it right. She didn't want to risk the commission she'd get from a sale. She was only tolerating him for his money, only playing her game.

Just as he played his.

After all, it was money—and what he could do with it—that had brought him back to town in the first place. And it was time he got down to business, instead of staying on the road penned up in a car with a woman who made him feel like a sex-starved teenager again.

Would everyone think the way Tess did? Instead of being impressed by his wealth, would they only want what they could get of it? Maybe that was why Ben Sawyer had played that coming-home-to-your-roots angle with him.

All week, the things Ben said to him had run around in his thoughts. Why would Ben—or anyone else in Flagman's Folly—have any other reason to care if he stayed around?

Ben had been one of the town's heroes, along with Paul Wright. Ben, the boy voted Most Likely to Succeed, and Paul, the football team's star quarterback.

He hadn't played any sport at all. Or done anything to show he might someday become a success in any area. He'd had no money, no charm. No claim to fame.

Unless you counted having a mama who made headlines like the one he'd once found scrawled in black marker with his own telephone number below it on the men's room wall at the Double S.

For a good time, call Mary Cantrell.

CALEB REALIZED his great plan to stay in town to talk with folks—to keep from going off alone with Tess—had raised an issue he had never anticipated.

"Well," she said as they walked down the center aisle of the pharmacy, sacks in hand, "I think we've hit about every business in sight."

"Looks like it." Along with showing him around, she'd spread her business cards and brochures far and wide. "Not such a bad idea, after all. Maybe you'll get some new customers from the promo."

"If they even realize they have it," she said, sounding almost resentful.

"They all said they'd talk up your agency to anybody interested in a house."

"After that spending spree of yours, they'll probably forget where they put the brochures."

"I did buy the stores out, didn't I?"

"Close enough." She hefted one of the sacks she carried. "Did you really need fifteen razors?"

"Gifts for the ranch hands back home."

"How thoughtful."

"I'm a thoughtful man. Didn't I offer to buy you that box of chocolates?"

She groaned. "Don't start on that again, Caleb, please. I told you, the flowers and dishtowels for Mom and the pie tins for Aunt El were enough."

"Think your aunt will try them out soon?"

"How should I know? Let's get this latest haul of yours to the car, shall we? *If* we can find another spare inch to stow it."

He grinned. She hadn't wanted him to buy the gifts. He'd expected that.

As she turned away, his grin faded.

The walking and the many trips to Tess's car had shown him he wasn't ready yet for all this physical activity. As he'd told Ellamae, he felt his aches from time to time. Probably always would, the doctors had warned him, just as he'd always have the awkward limp when he got tired.

Today's pain didn't worry him too much, either.

The first time they'd exited a building and found his new pint-size fan girls in the vicinity, he'd had a feeling they'd stick around.

Sure enough, as he looked through the plateglass window of the pharmacy, he could see the group standing on the other side of the street.

"Oh, Nate," Tess murmured under her breath. She shook her head and pulled the door open.

"Come on," he said, taking her by the elbow. "We forgot to make a stop over here." As he led her toward the next building, he felt her arm stiffen. Had she planned to skip this last store?

He slowed his step, knowing he couldn't insist on her going inside. But he needed to make this one last stop, to take one final shot at following his plan. Because, all morning, he'd felt thrown by the reactions of everyone they'd come across.

He'd wanted to show folks that money meant nothing to him, because he had plenty. But they'd appreciated his purchases. And they seemed more interested in talking with him about everything from the upcoming Fourth of July parade to their opinions of the politics of Flagman's Folly.

It hadn't made a bit of sense.

Tess stood staring at him. After a moment, she continued forward, and he fell into place beside her.

When they reached the automatic sliding doors of the building, she gave a little sigh.

As if in sympathy, a collective gasp rose from the opposite sidewalk. His fan girls exchanged looks of dismay and rushed into a huddle.

He smiled. What were they up to now?

Not waiting to find out, he walked with Tess into the air-conditioned coolness of Harley's General Store.

TESS FROZE. And not just because they'd turned the corner into the freezer aisle of the store, either.

She hadn't wanted to come in here, hadn't wanted to meet with Joe Harley while Caleb stood by her side. Until they'd talked to the clerk at the front register, she'd held out hope that Joe had business somewhere else this morning. But, no, there he was, kneeling in front of the frozen-food cooler, rearranging gallon-size tubs of ice cream. *Rocky Road.*

A perfect description of her life right now!

She could have argued about this meeting. And probably should have. But Caleb seemed determined to stop in at every business in town.

Including Harley's General.

Could his single-mindedness in coming here have something to do with Nate's little announcement at breakfast that first morning?

She shook off the idea. Sure, Caleb had asked her later if she planned to marry Joe. That didn't mean he cared about her. Or about any wedding plans she might—or might not—have. He had no reason to talk to Joe. But on second thought, better the two men should meet now, while she could be there to deflect the conversation away from subjects that shouldn't concern Caleb.

Joe had risen to his feet. Losing the battle to tug his blue smock closed, he gave up and held out his hand. "Well, now, Caleb. Heard you were back in town. It's right nice seeing you again, after all these years."

"Thanks. Same here." Caleb gestured. "I'm staying with Tess."

Joe frowned.

"You're *a guest* at the *bed-and-breakfast,*" she said between clenched teeth, giving Caleb the coldest look she could manage.

"Right. That's what I said. Your house."

Joe looked at her, then back at Caleb. "You planning on staying long?"

Caleb's mouth curved slowly in a half smile.

The sudden shiver that ran through her didn't come from seeing that. No, it was from all the frosty air billowing out from the cooler. She reached over and smacked the door closed.

"Don't have a definite departure date yet," he drawled in answer to Joe's question. "But, I'll tell you something. Tess's sweet rolls are so good, they might convince me to hang around a bit."

She swallowed a groan. "*My mother* made the rolls," she corrected.

"Did she? I thought you did."

"No. I'm too busy selling real estate, remember? Or trying to." She turned away from him. "Which is why we're here today, Joe." She explained about the brochure for Wright Place Realty.

"Well, sure, I'll be happy to post one on the community bulletin board up front. In fact, give me a pile of them. And your cards, too."

His wide smile puffed up his face like a snowman's—appropriate enough considering their surroundings, but a poor contrast to Caleb's chiseled cheeks. She blinked, shoving the unkind thought from her mind even as she pushed a good number of brochures and business cards into Joe's outstretched hand. She might as well get something out of this humiliating situation.

"I'll pass these around at the next town council meeting."

"Thanks, I appreciate it."

He looked quickly at Caleb, then back at her again. "And we're still on for supper tonight, aren't we? It's Friday."

Caleb turned his head her way as if wanting to see as well as hear her response. She made sure to show him. She fastened her gaze on Joe, and said firmly, "Yes, we're still on. I'm looking forward to it."

A loud bang filled the air, followed by a child's high-pitched screech.

"Joe, breakage up front, aisle three," announced the clerk over the store's loudspeakers—and over the child's continuing wail. "That's Billie Jo's little one caterwauling. He's fine, but oh, my…we've got dill pickles bouncing *everywhere*."

"Excuse me," Joe said, backing away. "A store owner's work is never done. I'll pick you up at seven, Tess."

As Joe left, she turned to Caleb. "That was uncalled for."

He shook his head. "That's harsh, isn't it? I'm sure the man didn't mean to be rude. He had to go take care of his pickles."

She sighed. "Not funny. You know exactly what I meant—your remark about staying with me."

"Aw, you shouldn't let that upset you none. I'm sure

Joe's a very understanding man. Although, come to think of it, he did look a bit taken aback by the idea, didn't he? Doesn't he know about your mama's bed-and-breakfast? Maybe you should tell him at supper."

So, he *did* care that she planned to go out with Joe. Why? He had no right to interfere in what she did. He never would. She'd make sure of it. "Caleb Cantrell—"

"Tess LaSalle." He murmured her name, his voice low and husky, his exaggerated drawl long gone. He leaned forward until their bodies almost touched. "I am staying with you, aren't I? I'm even sharing your room—"

"You are not—"

"I am." He tilted his head down until their mouths almost touched, too. "I've got to be in your room, one way or another, if I'm in your dreams." He smiled. "Bet your good ol' pickle-picker-upper can't lay claim to *that* one."

"You're right," she said, keeping her voice low, as well. "Joe's no dream. He's a man that can be counted on." Shaking, she turned away, certain she'd had the last word. Knowing nothing could top the truth. And hoping Caleb had gotten the message.

He put his hand on her elbow. In the coolness of the frozen-food aisle, his fingers felt hot against her skin. She swallowed hard and tried even harder to keep from yanking her arm free. From letting him see how he affected her.

He opened his mouth, but before he could say a word, she blurted the most critical comment she could think of. "And at least Joe doesn't turn his down-home accent off and on."

He tilted his head again, putting his cheek close to hers. "Yeah," he breathed into her ear, "but I'll bet he doesn't turn you on, either."

A FEW MINUTES LATER, after saying their goodbyes to Joe, Caleb trailed after Tess, who stomped toward the front door of the store. She hadn't looked his way once since they'd left the ice cream section behind. Could he blame her?

He shook his head in amazement at what had happened back there.

His plan called for impressing Tess just the way he would drive home his message to the rest of the folks in town. It didn't involve teasing her. Or getting so close he could have kissed her. But his brain had had other ideas, and his body had followed along, same as that first night at the inn, when he'd stood in the upstairs hallway with her. Now, at last, he knew why—though it galled him to admit he'd have to credit the news of her date with old Joe for smartening him up.

He intended to rub everyone's noses in his wealth, to prove he was just as good as they were. But that wouldn't work with Tess. With Tess, he needed something more.

He wanted her to see what she had missed. To know just what she'd walked away from when she took off to marry some other guy.

And yeah, dammit, to realize he was the best thing she could ever have had.

A few steps ahead of him, she came to a dead halt just inside the automatic doors. His revelations had put so much kick in his stride, he barely reined himself to a stop in time to keep from trampling her.

As the doors slid open, he followed her gaze to the sidewalk outside, where his local fan club stood waiting.

"Not again," she muttered.

"Yep, again. Or still. And it seems like their numbers have swelled." They had additional reinforcements with them. Reinforcements that weren't so pint-size. "Your mama and aunt have joined them."

"They'd better not have." Her words sounded threatening. She barreled through the front doorway like a bull down the chute.

"Hello, *again*," she said to the crowd on the sidewalk.

Her forced cheerfulness couldn't have rung true to any of them, yet they all smiled back as if she'd meant it.

"And my," she went on, looking at the women, "isn't it nice to see you two here. But Aunt El, don't you have to go to work this morning?"

"We're on our way over to the Double S." Her aunt made a production of looking at her watch, then stretching her wrist out at arm's length. "Noon, see? I normally get a lunch right about now."

"The judge lets you off for good behavior?" Caleb asked.

The two older women laughed and glanced at each other.

Finally Tess made eye contact with him again—only to shoot him a look that told him she didn't appreciate his humor. Or, more likely, his interference.

"How did your morning go?" Roselynn asked.

"Fine." Tess clipped the word.

"Not bad," he said more easily. "Just a few visits to touch base with folks again."

Roselynn smiled. "That's good. Did they get you all caught up on things?"

"I don't know about that. They talked politics, mostly."

"Heck, that wasn't worth the trip," Ellamae assured him. "We've had the same mayor for years, and he was a shoo-in this time around, too. What else did you talk about?"

"Not a lot. We didn't have enough time for any real conversation."

Tess made a strangled sound. Probably thinking again about his spending spree.

"Is that so?" Ellamae looked at Roselynn, who smiled. Without their saying a word, he had the feeling they'd spoken volumes between them.

"Our visiting's done now, though." He turned to Tess. "We'll be heading out of town to look at property again, won't we?"

"Tomorrow," she confirmed.

"Then can we go to lunch with you and Gram, Aunt El?" Nate asked. "Caleb can come with us."

"No, I don't believe that will work," Tess said.

He registered the strain in her voice and guessed her thoughts had flown to how much a meal for this gang would cost.

No problem there. He'd willingly pick up the check. It would pay Dori and Manny back some for all they'd given him. But as he opened his mouth, Tess cut him off, just as she had at the store.

"Gram has your lunch ready at home," she told Nate.

"I'll eat it for supper," she shot back.

She looked on the verge of having a tantrum right there on the sidewalk. Tess looked about to explode. A gut feeling told him his arrival in town might have added to her parenting troubles. The thought made him feel low.

"Well," he said quickly, "we're here now, all together. Why don't we walk on over to the restaurant? My treat."

The girls cheered. The two women smiled.

Tess looked up at him. "How nice of you, Caleb." She'd muttered the words for him alone, and again her tone fell far short of matching her words.

"Just trying to be hospitable," he said. Besides, along

with adding to the profits of the Double S, he'd have been a fool not to grab this opportunity to show a few more folks the big spender he'd become.

The sour look she sent him—eyes squinted, lips pursed—made him think she'd seen right through to that last goal.

And that she didn't much like what she saw.

Chapter Nine

Tess had hoped for an empty table at the Double S—a nice, long table that would put distance between her and Caleb. She should have known Roselynn and Aunt El would immediately claim their favorite booth up front next to the window. From there, they could see both everything that went on in the café and anything that happened within sight on Signal Street.

With luck, nothing of interest would happen at their *own* lunch table. She had noticed the look they'd exchanged outside Harley's General Store. They were up to something, no doubt about it.

Uneasily, she followed her aunt across the room.

"I'm sitting next to Caleb," Nate announced.

"There's not enough room for all of us," Tess said before her daughter could put the statement into action. "You girls can take the next booth."

To head off any argument, she promptly dropped onto one of the bench seats and scooted over to the space near the window. She expected her aunt, who had hovered near her elbow, to follow. Instead, Aunt El gestured to Caleb.

Squaring her shoulders, Tess locked gazes with him. As strongly as she could without words, she attempted to send the idea that he'd do much better to choose a seat somewhere else.

He nodded, as if confirming receipt of her message. Then, just as she began to relax, he smiled, sat on the end of her bench, and slid across it nearly to the center.

"Well, thank you," Ellamae said, plopping down beside him. "Just give a gal a little more elbow room, would you?"

"Sure thing."

Caleb moved closer to Tess, close enough that she could feel the warmth radiating from him, the slight press of his thigh against hers.

His mouth had tightened into a straight line, but the skin around his eyes crinkled. The man was laughing at her. Was probably trying to unnerve her.

Gritting her teeth, she fought the idea of edging closer to the window. That would only give him proof of how well he'd succeeded.

Ridiculous. Here she sat at high noon, in a crowded café, in front of her entire family, and she was allowing this man to get to her.

To her dismay, her aunt waved again. "Come on over, girls. Plenty of room now. Nate, you settle there by your gram. Lissa, hop up beside her. The rest of you, pull up a couple of chairs and we'll be all set."

Tess swallowed a groan. Trust Aunt El to take over. But what could she say about it? Besides, her aunt's grin showed how pleased she felt at coming up with a solution she thought suited everyone.

Not quite.

Even more apprehensive now, Tess watched as Nate scrambled across the bench, eager to take the next-best place of honor—the seat opposite her hero.

As the rest of the group grabbed at menus, Tess rubbed her temple, feeling a monstrous headache coming on, all thanks to the man beside her. When she caught Caleb looking at her, she froze.

"Sun in your eyes?" he murmured sympathetically. "Want to switch places?"

The others were too busy to hear this side conversation. She looked pointedly from the booth's tabletop to the small space between them. "What do you plan to do," she muttered, "climb over me?"

The wicked gleam in his eyes made her flush. She hadn't meant anything by her sarcastic question except to vent her frustration. But that gleam and his soft laugh told her he'd found an underlying message in it.

Another great choice of words. Good thing she hadn't said *that* aloud, too.

"Whatever it takes, Tess." He dipped his head toward her, and his eyes looked suddenly serious. "That's a promise."

She laughed bitterly. "No, thanks. You can keep your promises to yourself." She didn't want anything to do with them.

"What *do* you want, Mom?"

Startled, she looked up to see Nate waving a menu at her.

"Everybody's ready but you and Caleb."

Oh, she was ready all right. To get him on the road again tomorrow and on the way to a sale that would take him out of her life. Their lives.

What he was ready for...

She recalled that gleam in his eyes and had a very good idea of what he had in mind. She didn't want that from him, either.

No matter what her dreams said.

She looked over toward the end of the booth, where Dori stood waiting to take her order. "I know what I'm having," she said, forcing a smile. "A bowl of Manny's good, hot chili."

"Act like it, too," Caleb muttered. "*Real* chilly."

"What?" she asked, struggling to keep her voice down in front of their witnesses.

"I said I'd like that, too." He smiled and turned away to place his order. "A bowl of real, homemade chili."

After Dori had gone back to the kitchen, the others returned to their conversation.

She slumped back against her seat and raised her hand to her temple again. "Caleb," she muttered, "why don't you just give me a break."

LUNCH HAD GONE DOWNHILL from there, in Tess's opinion.

Just as they had done ever since they'd met him, the girls hung on Caleb's every word. Worse, Roselynn and Aunt El did the same, while occasionally sending each other meaning-filled glances. Once in a while, they let their gazes slide her way.

They'd cooked something up between them. Who knew what—but one thing was certain. Aunt El had instigated the plan.

She would have an easier time dealing with Nate's belligerence than she would trying to get anything out of her aunt. Instead, she'd have to corner her mother.

Meanwhile, stuck beside Caleb in their booth, she was literally held captive for more of his rodeo tales. Did the man's stories never end?

Though she had to suffer through watching the adulation on Nate's face, at least she had the satisfaction of knowing the conversation didn't stray into any dangerous topics.

When their group left the Double S, Tess trailed behind, trying not to grumble under her breath.

Caleb held the door for her, and as she stepped outside, she saw everyone had gathered beside a car that had pulled to the curb. Kayla Robertson sat behind the wheel. Tess smiled. Kayla had lived in Chicago, but since marrying Sam last year, she had become a part of Flagman's Folly and Tess's good friend.

Their daughter's puppy hung his head through the rear passenger window. The dog, a Labrador-Shepherd mix, had a tan face, with one eye completely surrounded by dark fur.

"This is Becky's puppy," Nate told Caleb. "His name's Pirate. Becky can't hear, so she talks in sign language. This is how you say 'Pirate.'" She put her hand over her right eye.

"Like an eye patch," Caleb said.

"Right." Nate beamed at him.

Tess stepped forward and made introductions.

Kayla reached through the window to shake Caleb's hand. "I've heard a lot about you from Sam," she told him.

"Have you?" He seemed taken aback.

"Oh, yes. And he's heard you're in town again. He plans to be in touch."

"Where's Becky?" Nate asked.

"Home." Kayla laughed. "She's getting to be a real rancher. My sister's coming for a visit soon, and Becky's already excited about showing her aunt how she feeds the chickens. Her daddy and the ranch hands are going to build her a chicken coop one of these days. Now that the subject's come up," she said to Caleb, "I'll warn you Sam mentioned having you stop by the house." Her gaze shot toward the two older women and back again. "And once I tell him what Roselynn said about knowing your way around with a hammer and a paintbrush, you're doomed."

He grinned at her. "Any time. Just say the word."

Tess swallowed her frustration. Or tried to.

"I'd better get going," Kayla said. "I'm taking Pirate to the V-E-T."

"Is he sick?" Nate asked in alarm.

"No, just going for a checkup. Tess, call me." Kayla waved to them all, then pulled the car away from the curb.

Before anyone could move, Aunt El announced, "Well, we've got a busy day on the books for tomorrow."

Tess looked at her. "You mean at Town Hall?" she asked warily. Hopefully.

"You know I told the judge I don't work on Saturdays. That's family time."

She shook her head. "Sorry, Aunt El, I'm afraid I'm busy, too. Whatever you have planned, you'll have to count me out."

"Oh, sugar, that's a real shame," Roselynn murmured.

Her aunt stared steadily at her for a long moment. Then she drawled, "Why, that's not a problem, Tess. We can work around you. We just need this man standing by your side." She put both hands on her hips and grinned up at him. "It's high time we reintroduce Caleb Cantrell to the gentry of Flagman's Folly."

So *that's* what those two were up to. "Really, that's not necessary."

"It surely is."

"No, Mom," she said, trying not to sound as desperate as she felt. That would be all she needed, to have Caleb distracted from their business. Maybe to have him extend his stay. Just the thought made her shudder. "Caleb's here to look at property."

"Can't spend all our time doing that," he said.

"We don't have time to waste, either," she shot back, refusing to look at him.

"What's gentry?" Nate asked.

"Besides," Tess rushed on, feeling her control of the situation beginning to slip, "we've already lost today."

"Well, I don't see—"

"And I don't see why you have all this interest in visiting with folks."

"Why wouldn't I?"

He'd asked calmly enough, but from the corner of her eye, she saw him tense. She couldn't antagonize him now. She couldn't upset him at all.

Facing him, she said, "I thought you'd want to get your business taken care of so you can go back to Montana."

"What's gentry?" Nate asked again.

Tess sighed. "It means people. Gram and Aunt El want to introduce Caleb to folks."

"That's a great idea, Mom! We can help."

"Yeah." Lissa nodded. "We know lots of people."

"Good. You just hold on to those thoughts," Aunt El said cheerfully. "They're sure to come in handy. But for now, we've got plenty of things lined up."

"Yes," Roselynn agreed. "Starting with a potluck tomorrow afternoon at Ben Sawyer's place."

"Ben?" Tess asked. "He's invol—?" She caught herself, took a deep breath, and tried again. "I mean, he's invited us out to the ranch tomorrow?"

Smiling, Roselynn shook her head. "Not just us. The potluck's open to the entire town."

"Oh, that's great," Tess said brightly. As the others began walking up Signal Street, she added under her breath, "Just great."

Only Caleb hung back, looking down at her, his expression unreadable.

She frowned. "What?"

"You got something against potlucks?"

"No, not at all."

"You don't care for Ben Sawyer?"

"Of course I like Ben."

"Hey, Caleb," Nate yelled from several yards ahead. "You comin'?"

"Be right there," he called. He turned his attention back to her. "What it is, then? Something's bothering you about this *invitation*."

His emphasis showed he had picked up on the way she'd stumbled over her words. "Nothing's bothering me."

"Good. Then you ought to be happy about getting me out of your hair tomorrow. After all, you said you wanted a break." He turned and left her standing openmouthed on the sidewalk.

She clamped her jaw shut on the words that threatened to spill out this time. Then she shook her head.

If he thought he'd be going off to Ben's ranch without her tomorrow, he was in for a surprise. She didn't trust him alone long enough to have lunch with her family. She couldn't risk leaving him on his own with them all afternoon.

Darn it, why couldn't Ben Sawyer stay out of this? Why should he feel the need to get involved in anything to do with Caleb? And why hadn't he mentioned something to her about the potluck earlier this week—when she would have had time to set up any number of appointments to keep Caleb out of town?

She stole a glance up the street.

The group had stopped and stood waiting for Caleb.

The first thing she saw was the satisfied smile on Aunt El's face. And the first thing she realized was that Ben hadn't thought of the potluck all on his own. He'd had help.

She had no doubt whatsoever about just who had come up with the terrible idea.

Come to think of it, Kayla Robertson had looked to

Roselynn and Aunt El in the middle of her conversation. Sure, Sam might have intended to get in touch with Caleb. But that request from Kayla—for him to help build a chicken coop for their daughter, of all things—had come at a very opportune moment. Accompanied by her comment about Caleb's handyman skills, how could that request have been a coincidence?

It couldn't. Grinding her teeth in irritation, she looked at the crowd up ahead again.

Caleb stood head and shoulders above her mom and Aunt El and all the girls around him. He smiled and joked with them as if he didn't have a care in the world but to keep them entertained.

Well, of course.

He'd been stuck in a car with her almost the entire week while she'd taken him all over the state. He'd probably sat counting the minutes until he would have his audience around him again.

He laughed at something Aunt El said, then turned to listen to Nate.

The smile and the adoring look she gave him made Tess's stomach tighten. As she watched, he reached out and ruffled Nate's hair. Even from this distance, she could see the color rush to fill her daughter's face.

It was nothing compared to the flash of fear that shot through Tess.

Chapter Ten

What a week.

Tess slumped into her swivel chair and rested her head on her hands.

After lunch, Caleb had announced he needed a haircut. She had made sure to see Roselynn and Nate off to the inn in the company of all Nate's friends. Then she had escaped to her office, desperately seeking a few minutes away from everyone.

It had been bad enough to know she would have to sit down to every breakfast and supper with Caleb.

She hadn't anticipated how tough the times alone with him would be.

She had envisioned them firmly belted into their separate seats of her car. Or maybe outside, tramping over some of the property she wanted to show, with plenty of wide, open space between them. She hadn't thought about the long hours beside him in her small car, where the simmering attraction she felt for him only added to the heat inside the vehicle. Between the mileage and her need to turn up the air conditioner, she was spending a fortune on gas.

Yet being nearly glued to his side in front of everyone they'd met this morning had been worse.

And then lunch. After Caleb had offered to treat everyone, she had wanted to run away. But she couldn't risk leaving him alone with Nate. Or with Roselynn and Aunt El. So she had given in and gone along. And what a meal *that* had been!

The sound of footsteps on the hardwood floor of the office made her jump. She raised her head and found Dana eyeing her in concern.

"Are you all right?" Dana asked.

"I'm fine. I didn't hear you come in."

"I didn't. I was in the back office."

Despite her worries, the phrase made them laugh, as usual.

She looked around. Their two oversize desks took up most of the floor space in this storefront room that no self-respecting real estate agent could call anything but tiny.

Beyond the wall behind them lay a minuscule strip of footage their new building owner had dared to label a second office. They'd managed to fit in a drop-leaf table—with both leaves dropped. A two-drawer filing cabinet did double duty as a resting place for a minirefrigerator, a coffeemaker and a hot plate for their teakettle.

"The 'back office.'" She shook her head. "Ben ought to try selling houses for a living. He's got such a way with words, you should hire him."

"No, I should not." As if to underscore her emphatic response, Dana dropped into the chair beside Tess's desk. "You look done in. What's going on with you and Caleb?"

She jumped again. "Wh-what?"

"Caleb. You know, our client? The one you're showing properties to? How's it going?"

"Oh." She began rearranging the office supplies on the desktop. "Fine—except for today. He wanted to stay in town. We walked the length of the business area and back again, stopping in at every store and office along the way."

Dana frowned. "What for?"

She shrugged, recalling all he had told her but not feeling a bit certain he'd shared his real reason with her. "He said he wanted to see the sights. While we were at it, I took care of handing out our promo."

"That's good. We need to drum up some business."

"I know." Guilt ran through her yet again. At the feelings she shouldn't have for Caleb. At the secret she'd kept from him for so long. At the worry her refusal to show him property close to town would ultimately hurt her best friend.

The wasted day today had only increased her distress.

As if she had picked up on Tess's thoughts, Dana said, "You didn't go out of town with him, then?"

"We didn't even get off Signal Street."

"You've been doing your best. Just keep at it." Her eyes sparkling, Dana leaned forward. "Seems to me he's dragging his heels with you about looking at property. What's he up to?"

That's what *she* had asked him.

And now she had stirred Dana's interest—exactly what she needed to avoid. "Nothing much. He just wanted to relive old times, I guess."

"And catch up with you?" Dana asked. "That's what he said when he came in here that first day."

She hurried to change the subject. "Everywhere we turned, we found Nate and Lissa and crew waiting for us—no matter how often I tried distracting them with the idea of going somewhere else."

"He's certainly caught their eye."

"Uh-huh." She sure hadn't. He'd asked her about leaving Flagman's Folly the next day. Because he wanted to find his big, expensive ranch property.

Not because he wanted to be alone with her.

Why did that thought hurt so much? Especially when she didn't want to be alone with him, either. Not after that episode at the store. But she had to do something to get him out of town. Nate's reaction to him had proven that.

Roselynn and Aunt El had made her goal impossible, at least for tomorrow. Once Caleb had heard their grand plan to reintroduce him to folks at Ben's potluck, he seemed to have lost all interest in leaving town.

Glancing down, she swept a handful of paper clips from the desktop into her palm and clenched her fingers around them. "Having Caleb around Nate is the *last* thing I need right now," she muttered.

"Why?"

For a long moment, she sat frozen. Then she opened her fist and let the clips trickle into her pencil drawer. She had almost forgotten Dana, who now looked even more interested. Worse, she had almost slipped. Had come close to blurting out a truth her best friend had never known. One no one knew.

Easing the drawer closed, she searched frantically for a response that would take them off this dangerous topic. "Well...I'm having enough trouble with Nate as it is. We've always gotten along fine, always acted like two of a kind. But lately, she seems to go out of her way to disagree with every word I say."

"Lissa's the same. It comes with being a preteen. They have to go through that confrontational stage. We did, too."

"I suppose." She'd told herself that many times. But even armed with the knowledge, she'd been helpless to stop the tension between them. That shouldn't have come as a surprise. Much as she hated to admit it, her daughter's rebellious streak matched her own at that age—as her

FREE Merchandise is 'in the Cards' for you!

Dear Reader,

We're giving away FREE MERCHANDISE!

Seriously, we'd like to reward you for reading this novel by giving you **FREE MERCHANDISE** worth over $20. And no purchase is necessary!

You see the Jack of Hearts sticker above? Paste that sticker in the box on the Free Merchandise Voucher inside. Return the Voucher promptly...and we'll send you valuable Free Merchandise!

Thanks again for reading one of our novels—and enjoy your Free Merchandise with our compliments!

Pam Powers

Pam Powers

P.S. Look inside to see what Free Merchandise is **"in the cards"** for you!

W

e'd like to send you two free books to introduce you to the Harlequin American Romance® series. These books are worth over $10, but they are yours to keep absolutely FREE! We'll even send you 2 wonderful surprise gifts. You can't lose!

REMEMBER: Your Free Merchandise, consisting of **2 Free Books** and **2 Free Gifts**, is worth over $20.00! No purchase is necessary, so please send for your Free Merchandise today.

FREE MERCHANDISE VOUCHER

2 FREE BOOKS and **2 FREE GIFTS**

Please send my Free Merchandise, consisting of
2 Free Books and **2 Free Mystery Gifts**.
I understand that I am under no obligation to buy
anything, as explained on the back of this card.

154/354 HDL FMNT

Please Print

FIRST NAME

LAST NAME

ADDRESS

APT.#   CITY

STATE/PROV.   ZIP/POSTAL CODE

Offer limited to one per household and not applicable to series that subscriber is currently receiving.
Your Privacy—The Reader Service is committed to protecting your privacy. Our Privacy Policy is available online at www.ReaderService.com or upon request from the Reader Service. We make a portion of our mailing list available to reputable third parties that offer products we believe may interest you. If you prefer that we not exchange your name with third parties, or if you wish to clarify or modify your communication preferences, please visit us at www.ReaderService.com/consumerschoice or write to us at Reader Service Preference Service, P.O. Box 9062, Buffalo, NY 14269. Include your complete name and address.

NO PURCHASE NECESSARY!

The Reader Service - Here's how it works:

Accepting your 2 free books and 2 free mystery gifts (gifts valued at approximately $10.00) places you under no obligation to buy anything. You may keep the books and gifts and return the shipping statement marked "cancel." If you do not cancel, about a month later we'll send you 4 additional books and bill you just $4.49 each in the U.S. or $5.24 each in Canada. That's a savings of at least 14% off the cover price. It's quite a bargain! Shipping and handling is just 50¢ per book in the U.S. and 75¢ per book in Canada.* You may cancel at any time, but if you choose to continue, every month we'll send you 4 more books, which you may either purchase at the discount price or return to us and cancel your subscription.

*Terms and prices subject to change without notice. Prices do not include applicable taxes. Sales tax applicable in N.Y. Canadian residents will be charged applicable taxes. Offer not valid in Quebec. All orders subject to credit approval. Books received may not be as shown. Credit or debit balances in a customer's account(s) may be offset by any other outstanding balance owed by or to the customer. Please allow 4 to 6 weeks for delivery. Offer available while quantities last.

mom had seemed all too eager to tell their guest at break-fast that first morning.

As if she didn't have enough on her mind, now she had Caleb to contend with. Despair made her cheeks flush as she faced what she'd been trying to deny. His pres-ence made her more short-tempered. Stretched her nerves nearly to breaking point. And added a whole new layer of tension to her life.

A shiver rippled through her at the memory of their conversation alone at the store, ending with his cheek close to hers and his words whispered into her ear.

I'll bet he doesn't turn you on...

"—Caleb?" Dana asked.

"*No!* Not Ca—" She broke off in confusion. "What?"

Dana frowned. "What's gotten into you, girl? You'd said having Caleb around Nate was the last thing you needed. I repeat, what's Nate got to do with Caleb?"

"Everything."

"Really?" Dana looked more interested than ever.

She clutched the arms of her chair. "One major thing, anyhow. He might be off the rodeo circuit now, but as far as Nate and all the girls are concerned, he's still a walk-ing, talking reminder of it. They're more eager than ever to get to a rodeo. And you know what *that* means."

"I sure do. Money we don't have." She sighed. "Who knew we'd come to this, Tess?"

The office phone rang. Dana went to her desk to answer it. Tess held her breath, hoping this would be a call from a new client. A moment into the conversation, she could tell it wasn't.

She thought again of Dana's question. *Who knew we'd come to this?* She'd meant more than just their current fi-nancial dilemma, bad as it was. She was thinking about how different she'd expected her life to be. So had everyone else.

All the while they'd been growing up, even in high school, quiet, bookish Tess had been the one without a steady. Without boyfriends. Without any dates at all. Until...

Another topic she'd better stay away from.

Chatty, ready-to-be-liked Dana had been the one with a longtime steady. A boy who had always loved her. Who had become her husband and the father of her children.

And now Paul was gone.

Everyone in town had been touched by his death. Caleb had seemed affected by the news, too. She couldn't forget his stunned expression or the bleak look in his eyes when she'd told him. He'd probably never considered the idea of someone they knew—someone their age—dying.

Dana hung up the phone and stared out the front window for a moment. After a sigh, she looked at Tess and returned immediately to their previous conversation. "It bothers me, Tess, always having to deny our kids everything."

"We don't," she said earnestly. "It's only the extras we can't give them, and only for now. That will change. Soon."

"Yes, it will." Giving a decisive nod, Dana pushed herself away from her desk. "Just as soon as you make a sale to Caleb."

Tess slumped in her chair and tried to swallow her groan.

LATER THAT EVENING, after getting whupped by Nate more than once over a checkerboard, Caleb gave in and suggested they move outside for some fresh air. While she ran up to her room with the game, he went outside to the wooden porch swing.

Roselynn followed a moment later, carrying a tray with a couple of glasses and a pitcher of lemonade. "Thought you might like something to wet your whistle." She poured a glassful and handed it to him.

"Thanks." He took a sip of the drink. On the sour side, the way she'd discovered he liked it. The way he'd had to fight to keep from feeling tonight. Sour and cranky and...

Jealous.

While the rest of them had eaten their supper, Tess had gone off for her date with old Joe.

As Roselynn entered the house, Nate came out and took her usual seat on the porch. She leaned back against the railing, one leg stretched out across the front step.

The sun threw the lengthening shadow of a pine over them, cooling the air a little.

It had been a good while since their noon meal at the Double S. But not nearly long enough for him to forget Tess's attitude. Or her words.

He took another swig of his lemonade, trying to quench his thirst. And to drown his irritation.

When her aunt had announced the plan of having him get together with folks, Tess had shown all too plainly how little she liked the idea. And at lunch, she had outright told him to keep his promises to himself. She couldn't have made it any clearer that she didn't want anything from him. She didn't even want him around.

Hell, was she *still* ashamed to be in his company?

The thought riled him.

"Caleb, you're rich, aren't you?"

He started at Nate's question, unexpected in the quiet moment and unnerving in its bluntness. She had more than a little of her aunt Ellamae's personality in her.

When he looked across the porch, he found her with her head bent over her glass as if she were analyzing the contents. "Well…" He paused, wondering how to respond. Honesty ought to work. "I've got more money than some people have. And not as much as others."

"Do you have as much money as Mr. Harley?"

He rubbed the back of his neck. "I don't rightly know how to answer that. I wouldn't know how much money he has."

"Lots."

"Yeah, so I gathered." *Hand over fist,* Nate had said at breakfast the other day, quoting Ellamae. Then she'd added the man wanted to marry her mama. He thought she intended to pick up on that again now, but she threw another question at him.

"Are you dirty?" she asked.

He looked down at his jeans, then whacked his good knee with his free hand, brushing the fabric. "Nope, no dirt on me."

"Not *dirt*. Like, dirty rich."

He had trouble keeping his eyebrows from climbing. "I'm not sure I follow you."

"Aunt El says people who are dirty rich don't have a lick of sense."

"Oh." He smiled. "'Filthy rich,' you mean?"

"Yeah. Like I said."

"Uh-huh." Unable to help himself, he asked, "She was talking about me?"

"No." She shook her head so firmly, her curls bounced. "Aunt El says you've got plenty of sense."

He raised his cup to his mouth to hide another smile. The compliment pleased him more than it should have. Too bad Tess didn't have as good an opinion of him.

"She says you just need some direction."

Caught between a laugh and swallowing his lemonade, he wound up coughing. When he could finally catch his breath again, he asked, "Your aunt Ellamae said that to you?"

She shook her head again, her eyes hidden by her curls. "I listened in the hallway when she talked to Gram."

"I see." He sat there weighing his options.

First off, he could—and probably should—say something against her eavesdropping. He couldn't hold back a small smile, just imagining how Tess would take it if she learned he'd disciplined her daughter. And judging by Nate's chattiness, it wouldn't take long for Tess to find out.

At the same time, he hated the idea of stopping the flow of conversation—even if it made him feel like a heel for merely thinking about getting information from a nine-year-old.

He'd deal with the talking-to later. For now, curiosity won out.

"So…this filthy-rich person with no sense. Was your aunt talking about Mr. Harley?"

"No, somebody on TV."

"I see."

"But she said rich people look down on other people." She lifted her chin, finally making eye contact with him again. "You don't do that, do you?"

Now it was his turn to shake his head. If she'd only known the irony of that question… "No, I try not to look down on folks." Too bad everyone didn't do likewise.

"I figured."

"What's this all about, Nate? I mean, what's got you asking the questions? You feeling a need for money?"

"No. Mom and Gram are always talking about it." She shrugged. "But I was just wondering."

They sat there in silence.

A minute later, a dark green Chrysler came into view on Signal Street. He could see Joe and Tess inside. As Joe drove up to the bed-and-breakfast and turned into the drive leading around to the back, Tess waved. Nate returned the greeting with a definite lack of enthusiasm.

He frowned. "Nice to have your mama home," he offered.

"Uh-huh." She slumped back against the railing.

"Or not so nice?" he asked.

"She's always grumpy."

"And you're always in a good mood."

She glanced at him, then away again. "Most times," she mumbled.

They heard the slamming of the car's door. Seconds later, Joe turned the Chrysler back onto Signal Street and drove away. After a moment, Tess's footsteps crunched on the walkway.

Nate took a quick drink, wiped her mouth with the back of her hand, and said in a rush, "Are you gonna move here? 'Cause it's a really good place."

Another irony now.

He'd come back to Flagman's Folly only to do what he needed to leave it behind him forever.

He felt a sudden chill, cold as the ice-filled glass in his hands. Nate was already a self-confessed eavesdropper. Was she basing her questions on something she'd heard the adults say about him? He tried a smile. "You sound like your mama now. Next thing I know, you'll be wanting to sell me some property."

"But are you, Caleb?" She stared at him, her dark brown eyes unblinking and as serious as if everything in the world depended on his answer. "Are you gonna live here?"

The sound of Tess's footsteps grew louder. The steady rhythm of her shoes on the gravel walkway sounded like a clock ticking a countdown.

Leaning forward slowly, he set his glass on the tray Roselynn had left on a wicker side table. Then he rested his elbows on his knees and linked his fingers together in front of them. Finally, he looked again at Nate.

The eager look on her face told him the answer she wanted.

Honesty would have to work here, too.

"No, Nate. I just came back for a short while to visit. I don't belong in Flagman's Folly."

Tess turned the corner of the house. Their gazes met over the porch railing. Her dark brown eyes were as serious as Nate's.

But while her daughter's expression had looked full of hope, Tess's face couldn't hide her relief.

Chapter Eleven

Early the next afternoon, Caleb followed Tess and Rose-lynn across Ben Sawyer's yard.

After hearing Ellamae's news yesterday about the pot-luck at Ben's place, he'd looked forward to the chance for a relaxed, enjoyable meal.

Not that he had any complaints about the food at the Whistlestop. Roselynn's breakfasts and suppers more than satisfied his hunger. But the conversation sure had lacked something lately.

Last evening, it had been just the three of them. Nate had sat picking at her plate, wearing the most mournful look he'd ever seen on a child. Roselynn had caught on quick and spent most of her time going back and forth between the dining room and the kitchen.

At least whupping him at checkers had cheered the kid up.

Since coming back to the inn after her date, Tess had ignored him.

They took their places at the end of the line wending its way toward one of the trestle tables. The makeshift tables were loaded down with food, which pleased him no end.

"Looks like enough here to feed a couple of armies."

"It will go fast," Tess said.

"It surely will," Roselynn added. "Better take enough first time around, Caleb, so you don't get done out of it."

"No worries about that." They'd been here awhile now, and after more than a few conversations with folks already, he'd worked up an appetite.

He'd come today prepared as he always was when meeting with a crowd—same as he had with Nate and her friends—ready to regale them with tales of his rodeo days. To his surprise, he'd received responses similar to those he'd gotten in the shops on Signal Street. The folks of Flagman's Folly seemed less concerned about hearing his stories and more interested in welcoming him home.

He couldn't understand it.

The line shuffled forward and he followed, conscious of how close he stood to Tess. So close he could see a few tiny freckles on the back of her neck.

As he loaded potato salad and pickled beets onto his plate, he contemplated the situation with her.

Ever since their arrival, he'd expected her to put as much distance between them as possible. Yet except for helping Roselynn bring their contributions into the kitchen and later setting out the food, she'd stayed by his side nearly every minute. He couldn't understand that, either.

As he and Tess turned away from the trestle table now, he said, "Guess we're going to have a time finding somewhere to sit."

Before she could answer, Nate came running up. She and her friends seemed less inclined to hang around him today, probably due to all the games they'd had going on.

"Mom, do you know where Becky is? I can't see her anywhere."

"And you won't. The Robertsons aren't coming today. They already had plans to go up to Santa Fe."

"Oh, rats." Frowning, Nate stomped off.

Her mention of the Robertsons had jogged his memory. "It surprised me," he told Tess, "when you introduced me to Sam's wife outside the Double S yesterday. I didn't know he had a kid, either."

"Neither did he."

Raising his brows, he waited for her to say more, but she turned her back on him without another word. He could get that she put up defenses when they were alone out in the desert, when the heat of the day couldn't hold a candle to the heat between them inside the car—no matter how high she cranked up the air.

But even this afternoon, in front of other people, she had seemed to want nothing to do with him, had acted about as friendly as she had during their meals at the Whistlestop. So why was she sticking to him like a burr under a horse's saddle?

Again, he scanned the area. Ben definitely had invited a crowd.

A good thing, too. With so many people around, he hoped eventually to get his distance from Tess. Something he sorely needed. Any time he got near her, he couldn't help trying to get a rise out of her. And he always succeeded. But he had a feeling one of these times his teasing would come back to bite him.

If it hadn't already.

He hefted the plate of food in his hands and looked around again.

"Caleb. Over here!" Ellamae waved at them from a group of lawn chairs near one corner of the house.

As he headed across the yard, Tess fell into step beside him. It wasn't until he'd gotten closer to Ellamae that he saw who had taken one of the chairs—an older man with a tanned and wrinkled face and snowy white hair arranged in a style that would've looked good on a country singer back in the Fifties.

Judge Baylor.

Too late to back out now. Caleb gripped his paper cup of punch and tried to smile. Tess took one of the vacant lawn chairs. He set his food on the other one and reached down to shake hands with the judge.

"Didn't think y'all would miss the festivities," the man drawled, focusing on the pile of chicken wings on his overflowing plate. "I'll say one thing for Ben Sawyer. He does know how to entertain in style." He chomped down on a wing and grunted in approval.

Then, true to Caleb's memory of the judge, he proceeded to talk at length while the rest of them ate.

Caleb dug in to his potato salad.

Beside him, Tess pushed the food around on her plate, much as Nate had done last night and again this morning.

After a while, Judge Baylor wound down, took a long swig of sweet tea and sat back in satisfaction. Caleb found himself being inspected from head to foot, as if the judge had just seen him for the first time. "Well, now, aren't you a sight to behold."

He tensed. "That supposed to be a compliment, Your Honor?"

The judge's eyes narrowed. "Yes, son, I do believe it is. In any case, you're looking considerably better than the last time I saw you."

"You remember that far back?"

"Why, it wasn't that long ago. You were trussed up like a side of beef in that hospital bed you spent so much time in."

Startled, Caleb grabbed the plate that had begun to slide from his lap. "You're saying you saw me in the hospital? In Dallas?"

"You spent time in any other one since I've known you?"

He shook his head.

"That would be the place, then. You were an awful sight. Though I must say—" the judge's bushy brows—the same snowy white as his hair—lowered in a frown "—you keep on with that high-and-mighty tone of yours, I might find your inability to converse back then a marked improvement over today."

"Sorry," he muttered. "I've had a lot on my mind."

"I'll bet," Ellamae murmured. She put the last bite of her hamburger into her mouth and eyed him as she chewed.

Tess kept her attention glued to her plate.

Obviously neither of them planned to rush to his defense.

He focused on the older man again. "I never knew you'd come to Dallas."

"Yep. Me and Sam Robertson both. We'd heard the news on the television, of course, but folks in town wanted to know firsthand how you were doing."

He had to struggle to find his voice. "No one told me you'd visited."

"That's understandable. We didn't leave our calling cards." The judge picked up another chicken wing. "The nurse said they had you knocked out and you'd stay that way for a while and likely not get up to much when you came to."

"It might have been days before they would ease back on the medication, the nurse told them," Ellamae said, taking over the story. "So Sam and the judge turned tail and came back home again. They'd seen enough to tell everyone how you were doing."

"Poorly," the judge stated.

Hell of an understatement, there. "Yeah, that's a stretch of time I'd just as soon forget."

From the corner of his eye, he saw Tess shift, stabbing her fork into a pile of potato salad she hadn't yet touched.

"Ellamae, you're needed!" called one of the women from over near the house.

She waved in answer and began to struggle out of her lawn chair. "Well, you two just go on reminiscing about old times. Tess, you come along with me. I'm sure whatever's up over there, they can use an extra pair of hands."

Tess hesitated as if doubting she ought to leave. He frowned once again. Did she think he needed a guard? When she found him staring at her, her cheeks flushed pink and she staggered to her feet. The plate of salad nearly went flying.

As the two women hurried away, the judge turned back to Caleb. "Quite a few folks have said you've stopped in to visit with them in town."

"Yeah," he said, grinning. "We hit Signal Street. Tess said I'd gone on a real spending spree."

The judge shrugged. "Didn't hear anything about that."

Caleb stopped grinning and looked at him suspiciously. "No one mentioned it at all?"

"No. Just said it was good to see you again."

"Huh." Lost in thought, Caleb gathered up his own plate and his empty punch cup. Judge Baylor knew everything that happened in this town. Why hadn't he heard the news?

"Sit back, boy, take it easy." The judge waved his hand lazily. "No sense rushing off just yet. I don't see anybody starting up with the horseshoes, like at Sam Robertson's place." He sounded disappointed.

"I wouldn't know about that." But he could sure envision the older man flinging horseshoes with the same energy he used to throw out sentences in his courtroom.

"No, you never were at any of the Robertsons' barbecues, were you?"

"We weren't that friendly," he said, intending to leave it at that. But his tongue overrode his good sense. "I can't think why Sam would have come to see me in Dallas. Or you, for that matter, Your Honor."

He nodded. "Yeah, that was a good part of your problem all along. You couldn't think."

"I didn't need to." The paper plate crumpled as he tightened his grip. "Everybody in town made it obvious what *they* thought."

The judge grasped the arms of his lawn chair to pull himself upright. He leaned forward, his expression grave. Instead of the heated glare Caleb remembered from the past—and expected now—he found the man staring at him with something like compassion in his eyes.

"We watched you with some concern, true," the judge said. "Couldn't have been easy, growing up with a mama who gave her favors away like yours did."

Caleb narrowed his eyes. "You don't hold anything back, do you, Your Honor?"

"I did then. You're man enough to hear it now. And I'll say it again. You didn't think much in those days." He rose from his chair. "Folks saw you as a boy with a bad home life and—no surprise—a bad attitude to match." He shook his head. "What worries me now, son, is it seems like getting thrown from a bull and cracked to pieces still hasn't knocked that chip off your shoulder."

ONCE THE FUROR in Ben Sawyer's kitchen had calmed down, Tess could finally make out why her aunt had received such an urgent summons. The women had required her services to settle an argument over the proper way to prepare nuts for a pie. She had to smile. In her own way,

Aunt El held just as much power in this town as Judge Baylor did in his courtroom.

"Looks like my help's not needed, after all," she said to no one in particular. "I'll just slip back outside…"

On the porch, she stood and shook her head at herself. Maybe she had misjudged Aunt El. She and Roselynn had a long history of butting into things that didn't concern them. It hadn't taken much of a stretch to wonder whether, for some reason of her own, Aunt El had used the trip to the kitchen as an excuse to get her away from Caleb and Judge Baylor. Had she let the knowledge of her aunt's reputation color her judgment?

What about her suspicions of Caleb? Why *had* he come back to town? With his off-again, on-again interest in property, she was beginning to doubt his claim about wanting to buy a ranch. The thought of *not* making a sale to him made her hands suddenly clammy.

The fear of what he might really be up to made her entire body break out in a sweat.

She recalled what she'd overheard him saying to Nate last night. What he'd deliberately wanted her to overhear, she was sure. *I don't belong in Flagman's Folly.*

The memory of those words made her heart ache.

He had probably always felt that way, and she'd never realized it. He'd left town—and left her—because of it. Hadn't he said so, that night outside Gallup when she'd gone to find him? More words to make her heart ache.

All he'd worried about was his prize. His fame.

That's what's important. That's what will save me from going back to some one-horse town with one-horse folks in it.

Even back then, ten long years ago, he'd felt too good to stick around. Too good to be with her.

Shaken by those thoughts, she descended the porch

steps and forced her gaze to the corner of the house. Then she froze. The lawn chairs now had new occupants. She ground her teeth in frustration. Regardless of Aunt El's intent, she'd managed to separate her from Caleb. Where was he?

"Tess?"

She started at the sound of her name and found Ben Sawyer standing beside her. "Sorry, I didn't see you."

"Obviously. Looks like you have something on your mind. You had a heck of a scowl on your face, too."

"I was just squinting. The sun's so strong today."

"Uh-huh. Everything okay in the kitchen?"

"Yes, fine. And there's still plenty of food, too. The women of Flagman's Folly won't let you down."

"They do things right, don't they? Why do you think I had this potluck?"

So much for getting away from her suspicions. And he'd just asked a loaded question. "Why did you, anyhow? What made you decide to have the potluck today?"

He shoved his hands in his back pockets and shrugged. "It's been a while since I hosted a get-together for folks."

"Uh-huh. And who suddenly reminded you of this long passage of time? Were you by any chance chatting with Aunt El?"

"Yeah, I saw her here earlier on—"

"No, I meant before today. Did she put you up to this?"

"Huh?" He blinked.

She laughed. "Come on, Ben. You handled much tougher questions on the sixth-grade debate team. Aunt El talked you into having this potluck, didn't she?"

No answer.

She had opened her mouth to repeat the question when she noticed him staring across the yard. She'd lost him completely. Something else had caught his attention. Or someone. She turned to look, too.

Out by the roadside past the other parked vehicles, she spotted a new arrival. Dana's blue van.

She smiled with relief. When she'd mentioned the potluck to Dana yesterday afternoon, her friend had shown an odd reluctance about committing. Tess had done her best to convince Dana to come. She'd kept to herself too much since Paul's death. It wasn't good for her or for her kids.

Nate's friend Lissa now hurried away from the van with her four-year-old brother tugging to get out of her grip. But she held him tightly by the hand as she towed him toward the rowdy group of kids playing in a shady corner of the yard.

Dana appeared around the end of the van. In one hand, she balanced a casserole. With the other, she struggled to push her baby's stroller over the uneven ground.

Before Tess could move a step, Ben muttered, "'Scuse me."

He took off across the yard, his ground-eating stride indicating *he* was the one with something on his mind now. But even from here, Tess could see the less-than-welcoming expression on Dana's face.

She groaned. Now what? No matter how she tried to ignore the friction between her best friend and their landlord, it seemed evident that trouble was on the horizon.

And speaking of trouble…where was Caleb?

IF IT WASN'T one thing, it was another.

Ellamae shook her head as she herded her sister across Ben's yard to a quiet spot for a quick private chat. She'd finally gotten the argument in the kitchen straightened out when Roselynn had pounced.

"Ellamae," she started in again now, "I don't know that we're doing the right thing. I just saw Caleb, all alone and looking like a thundercloud, stalking off."

"He left?" She hadn't expected that.

"No, he went out past the barn."

"Oh, well. That's no worry. He probably wanted to look over Ben's horses." She grinned at her sister. "Loosen up a little, Rose. Don't want folks thinking something's up." After watching Roselynn force her lips into a stiff smile, she continued, "Tess and I left him with the judge, and I imagine the man said something to him he didn't take to. You know how blunt the judge can be."

That earned a small but genuine smile from Roselynn. "And you're not?"

"Never mind that. Where did Tess get off to?"

"I don't know. I thought she was with you. That's why I came looking." She sighed. "I saw her earlier, as well, and she didn't seem any too happy, either."

"She didn't eat a bite when we were chowing down with the judge."

"Again? She hasn't been eating a thing at home, either. El, she's breaking her heart over Caleb a second time."

"You should've seen her when they were talking about Caleb being in the hospital."

Roselynn shook her head. "She never would look at the news whenever they talked about him. Or read the articles in the paper. What are we going to do?"

"Just what we said we'd do. What we *are* doing. Getting him out and about with folks."

"But that's not helping Tess."

"It will. Give it some time. You're about as impatient as Nate."

Her sister's face softened in a smile. "She does have a case over him, doesn't she?"

"She sure does. Uh-oh," Ellamae muttered, "here comes Dana. She's not acting too happy, either. What is it with these young'uns? They're all looking sorrier than wet hens and behaving about as cheerful. Brace yourself. And mind what you say to her. Well, hello there, Dana," Ellamae said, pitching her voice to be heard clear out past the barn. "And how are you on this beautiful day?"

"I could be better," she said, her tone grim. "But it's not me I'm worrying about right now, thank you."

"The children?" Roselynn asked in alarm.

"Oh, no, they're fine. It's Tess and Caleb I meant. There seems to be some tension between them."

"Do you think so?" Roselynn asked.

"Can't say as we've noticed." Ellamae met her sister's gaze and held it. "Well, Rose, we've got to get back to the kitchen." She moved forward, only to have Dana sidestep in front of her, blocking their escape route.

"Just spare me a minute, ladies," Dana said, and it didn't sound like a request. "I've got a feeling there's something we need to discuss."

Chapter Twelve

Out by Ben's barn, Caleb stood with one foot braced on the bottom rung of the fence.

No one had come racing after him, surrounding him, clamoring for his autograph, wanting to take his photo. He wasn't the star of the show today, wasn't even in the running. That didn't quite fit his plan. But he couldn't seem to do anything to change it.

Folks treated him as though he'd always been around.

Maybe he should never have left town.

The idea—and what went with it—froze him in his seat.

Would he really go back to that time and place if he could? Back before the rodeo and the buckle bunnies and the fall that had brought him down from a bull one last time? The fall that had ended his career permanently?

Back to when he was nothing but the son of the good-time girl of Flagman's Folly, New Mexico?

He breathed in the good scent of the horses that stood in the corral, twitching their tails at annoying flies and occasionally neighing as if they were talking with him.

A much nicer conversation than the previous one he'd had, when the judge had gotten the last word by throwing out that accusation about his attitude when he was a teen.

He would have called the man on it—if he hadn't

been so taken aback over the rest of what the judge had told him.

He gripped the top fence rail as he recalled his first day back in town, when he'd stopped in at the Double S before going to find Tess. Then, Dori said the judge had contacted the hospital for news about his condition. Judge Baylor himself had confirmed that and more.

If he could believe everything the man had told him—

"Caleb?" Tess's voice, sounding uncertain, interrupted his thoughts.

When he turned his head, he found her standing by the corner of the barn, looking as tentative as she'd sounded and as young and nervous as…as that time outside Gallup.

Almost subconsciously, his hands tightened on the rough wood. But a second later, she strode over to stand beside him and rested her hand on the rail with an assurance that somehow irritated him.

He couldn't resist the chance to unsettle her. Maybe because he felt so ill at ease himself. "Miss me?" he asked, forcing a smile.

She frowned. "Let's say I wondered where you'd gone off to. You seemed a little shell-shocked over what the judge told you."

He laughed shortly. "And you didn't hear the half of it."

"What else did he have to say?"

Without thinking about it, he shrugged, then froze in position for a second. Exactly which shoulder did the judge think he had a chip on, anyway? "Nothing important. He likes to hear himself talk."

"You really didn't know he and Sam went to the hospital to see you?" The skin around her eyes crinkled as if she felt pain.

He had to look away. Inside the corral, a filly shook her head and snorted at a persistent fly.

"Never heard a thing about it. No big deal. I wasn't in shape for visitors, anyhow."

"I'm sorry for all your suffering," she murmured.

It was the first time she'd come straight out with her sympathy. He wasn't sure how to take it. Didn't want to take it at all.

Could he accept the opportunity she seemed to be offering, the chance to tell her everything he'd gone through in those long months in the hospital and the even longer months in rehab?

No, he didn't want sympathy. But the prospect of telling her what no one else knew, well, that was tempting.

He could tell her the things that bothered him most.

How close he'd come to dying.

And how sometimes, in the middle of the night when the pain ate at him and he fought taking his pills, how little the thought of that scared him.

He let go of the fence and shoved his hands in his back pockets. Took a deep breath and let it out an inch at a time.

"No big deal," he said again. "I got through it."

THE SETTING SUN cast a deep red tinge over the barren landscape around them. Running the back of her hand across her forehead in frustration, Tess scowled at the horizon and tried to ignore the man by her side.

They'd been together all day, something she certainly hadn't been able to claim in the week following Ben Sawyer's potluck. She'd spent most of her time asking herself the same question she had faced that day: where was Caleb? As hard as she tried to keep an eye on him, he somehow kept slipping from her grasp.

Between Aunt El's social calendar and Roselynn's list of odd jobs around the bed-and-breakfast, he stayed busier than she did. They'd barely had any time alone together.

On the one hand, she counted herself lucky. On the other hand, his full schedule didn't do anything to help her speed his departure.

She had finally put her foot down. Working around his *additional* social engagements, they'd managed to carve out some time during this second week to do what he'd supposedly come here for.

Part of her wondered whether her mom and Aunt El were solely to blame for everything. The other part of her suspected Caleb had purposely avoided being alone in her company.

At one point on the day of Ben's potluck, when she had finally tracked Caleb down near the barn, she'd thought for a moment he was going to open up to her. Was going to give them the chance to get close again.

And damn her, despite all the reasons she shouldn't even think about getting close to him, she wanted it.

She plucked at the neckline of her peasant blouse, pulling the soft fabric away from her in an effort to cool herself. The air had become much too warm for comfort. Or maybe she felt overheated because Caleb stood much too close.

"That's enough sightseeing for today," she said abruptly. "It's getting late."

"Sounds good to me." He started toward his rented pickup truck.

She followed, stopping just short of muttering under her breath. What she'd really meant was, she didn't have the energy—or the patience—to keep playing the role of tour guide.

She desperately needed a day off from everything and everyone. A day away from the long list of grievances about her life.

Her situation with Nate had gotten worse than ever.

She had done nothing to earn Dana's faith in her ability to make a sale to Caleb. She hadn't even come within a mile of getting him to make a preliminary offer.

Every chance she could, she had taken him around the state, showing him the available ranches and acreages on her listing. Every one of which he had found reasons to turn down.

Every one of which brought them in closer and closer to the outskirts of Flagman's Folly.

When she reached the truck, he opened the passenger door for her. She stood beside him, hesitating. She needed to make a sale. To get him out of town, away from Nate. Pushing a stray lock of hair from her forehead, she fought to keep the frustration from her voice. "You haven't seen anything yet that interests you?"

"I wouldn't exactly say that." He grinned down at her.

"Very funny. Too bad I couldn't *hold* your interest." The minute she'd spoken, she wished she hadn't.

But wishing wouldn't bring the words back, any more than longing for Caleb had brought him home to her. Ten years too late didn't count.

Besides, he hadn't returned to town for *her,* anyway.

His grin faded, but he continued to look down at her, his green eyes sparkling like sunshine on glass. "Tess—"

"Never mind."

Her cheeks burning, she stepped up into his truck and let him close the door behind her. As he walked around to the driver's side, she waved her hands furiously, hoping to cool her face. Maybe he'd think her flush had come from the setting sun.

He'd insisted on bringing the truck these past few days. Knowing the price of gas and the amount of territory she planned to cover, she hadn't said a word. Why couldn't she have held her tongue a minute ago, too?

And she'd thought Dana was the chatty one!

When he opened the driver's door, she clenched her hands into fists and dropped them to her sides. Breath held, she waited for him to start the truck. He didn't. Instead, he turned to her.

Her throat tightened, trapping the air in her chest.

He exhaled heavily, as if he'd held his breath, too. "You don't know how much I wish things had been different."

"Wishing doesn't get you anywhere." Hadn't she just acknowledged that? "And I don't want to talk about the past."

"You haven't made that hard for me to figure out."

"You didn't make things easy for me by leaving." Mentally chastising herself, she turned her head away. Why couldn't she stop blurting out the wrong things?

He reached up to touch her cheek, so gently she could barely feel his knuckle against her skin. Still, she flinched. But he'd managed to get her to face him again. Just as he'd succeeded in setting off her anger once more, stirring up the resentment that had bubbled inside her for days now. For years.

"I tried to see you before I left town," he said.

As if she could believe that. "Did you?"

"Yeah, I did. Went by your house to tell you goodbye. That made the second and last time I ever saw your granddaddy, when I rang the bell and he came to the door and said you were out."

She wouldn't have gotten any word he'd left for her. But she had to know. "Did you…leave a message?"

"Not likely, when he shut the door in my face." His voice had hardened. "Besides, what was I going to say? He didn't know about us."

"He did, once I got back from Gallup," she said grimly. "He told me I was wasting my time chasing after you."

She wouldn't tell Caleb a single detail about how her life had gone after that. Not for a million-dollar sale.

"He was right."

She stared, unable to speak. Unable to believe how much his words had hurt.

"Where were you going to get with me, Tess? Nowhere. You knew that well enough not to tell folks about us. You knew the way everyone looked down on me. I was the poorest kid in town."

Understanding washed through her. Compassion, too. He'd directed those hurtful words at himself, not at her. "No," she protested. "That wasn't why I didn't tell anyone. It didn't matter to me how much money you had."

"Whatever the reason, I don't blame you. Folks didn't want to bother with someone like me, with a mama no one could be proud of. Without a daddy even willing to give me his name."

At his last words, she clutched the armrest by her side. He was hitting much too close to home, if only he knew it. And she was coming much too near to doing something she should never do—telling him what was in her heart. In their history.

She could see the pain in his face, could hear it in his voice. She had to will herself to remain still and not reach out to him.

"At least leaving got me away from everyone's pity. And worse." He spoke so quietly, she could barely hear him.

"People knew your mother…slept around. And yes, some of them pitied you, Caleb," she said, her throat so tight she had to whisper the words. "Some of them thought less of you, too. But not everyone."

"Did you?"

She shook her head.

He looked at her, his eyes gleaming even in the now-dusky light. "If that's so, then maybe we ought to go back to where we were."

Her throat tightened another notch. What was he saying? That he'd had wishes about their relationship, too? Regrets about how it had ended? No. She couldn't let herself believe in that. Things could go just as wrong again as they had years ago, and now she had so much more to lose.

Still, she couldn't stop herself from blurting, "Back—" she had to clear her throat and fight to keep her tone neutral when she was racing out of control inside "—to the last time I saw you, you mean?"

"No, to where we left off before I went away. We had good times together. We had fun."

We had a baby.

No, she couldn't say that. He'd tossed out an apology not long ago, one she couldn't accept. Just as now she couldn't let him so high-handedly toss aside what they did have when they were together. "We had more than fun."

"Yeah, we did. I was getting to that." He paused, looked away for a moment, then brought his gaze back to hers. "I'd have come back home again, too. But you told me you were getting married—"

"And I'm sure you didn't stay lonely too long."

He gave her a half smile. "You *are* thinking about the last time you saw me, aren't you?"

"No, I'm not." She swallowed her rising panic. "I'm just…just wondering how things went for you after that. I know you found fame and fortune, but did you learn a lot from the rodeo life? Did you enjoy moving from place to place, living on the road?" She was babbling, but anything was better than letting the conversation head in the direction he'd been taking it. "Did you like all those girls hanging on you?"

She swallowed a groan. That wasn't where she'd meant to head, at all.

And darn him, this time he laughed outright.

"Buckle bunnies are part of rodeo. No living without them."

Just what did that *mean?*

Better not to ask. Probably better not to open her mouth again. Ever.

Still, she couldn't stop her surge of anger. He had seen right through her. Her thoughts *had* focused on the day she had tracked him down.

And the girls hanging on to his arms.

Irritation spilled out of her. "You certainly didn't feel hounded by your groupies back then!"

His eyes glinted. From the last rays of the sun as it made its way to the horizon? Or from more amusement he couldn't hide?

"No need to get in an uproar over it," he said. "Those girls were just wanting to hitch their wagons to the nearest star."

She exhaled forcefully. "Well, let me tell you something. I have never thought of you as 'Caleb Cantrell, rodeo star.' And I don't plan to start thinking that way now."

"You don't?"

She'd responded honestly and openly, not stopping to analyze a thing. If she'd thought twice, she might have held back, knowing her words would have to upset him. Yet the expression on his face now looked anything but upset.

The look in his eyes made her head swim. She had to tear her gaze away.

And at that moment, with that brief loss of contact,

in that tiny little window of time when she let down her guard and allowed her true feelings to show, she realized she'd contributed to her own undoing.

Before she could react, Caleb slipped his hand behind her head and gently urged her to turn toward him again. When she did, she found his face close to hers, their mouths only inches apart.

She tensed her hands, planning...wanting...*needing* to push him away. But after the past weeks of nerves stretched to the breaking point and the past ten years of unfulfilled wishes and destroyed dreams, she needed this just as much.

The chance to kiss Caleb.

No.

The chance to have Caleb kiss her, to let him realize what he had done and how he had hurt her and everything he had missed—and then the best chance of all, for her to tell him to *kiss off.*

That's what she needed.

But instead of moving forward as she expected, he leaned back. And brushed his finger teasingly along her skin just above the elastic neckline of her peasant blouse. Her heart began to pound.

Again, he did the unexpected. Instead of touching her mouth with his, he dipped his head. He brushed his warm lips against the fluttering pulse point below her ear, slid his finger beneath the elastic and eased the neckline aside to travel a path along her collarbone. She traveled, too, back to the time he'd discovered that very sensitive place on her body. The first time *she'd* known about it herself.

The reminder made her freeze in place.

And now, finally, his eyes dark and glittering, he leaned close and kissed her. The weight and heat of his mouth against hers made her heart race even faster.

She raised her hands to his chest, longing only to pull him against her, to relive the closeness they'd once shared. But the knowledge of what had happened between them then—what she had to prevent him from discovering now—told her she couldn't cuddle against him. Couldn't risk letting him take her into his arms. She had to push herself away from him.

But could she?

Chapter Thirteen

Caleb let Tess's words replay in his head.

I have never thought of you as 'Caleb Cantrell, rodeo star.' And I don't plan to start thinking that way now.

For once, he didn't have a lick of trouble with her outspokenness.

He'd never tell her that, or let her know how relieved she had made him feel. Or admit that her words had made everything right for him.

She flattened her palms against him, and the deep breath he took made his chest swell. With pride or contentment that she still wanted him, he didn't know. *Could she still want him?*

The question managed to slap some sense into his head.

What he was doing here was crazy.

When he and Tess had been together before, they were kids. They were adults now. Consenting adults. That knowledge *should* have provided the go-ahead to do what he wanted. And what was he doing? Behaving like a randy teen with his first crush, about to go too far in the front seat of a pickup truck.

A truck he didn't even own. Somehow, that made it worse.

Tess didn't deserve this.

Out of respect for her, he needed to stop.

In the same instant Tess pressed her palms against his chest, he leaned back and slid his arms from around her. Ignoring the twinge in his knee, he slid across the bench seat and behind the wheel again.

Damn. He'd come here to make things right for himself. Not to do everything wrong.

It was dark enough now inside the cab of the truck that he couldn't see Tess's face. Good. That meant she couldn't see his. He made a fist and tapped the side of it lightly on the dashboard. Then he started the pickup. "Time to head back," he muttered.

Silence.

"Got a little carried away there."

More silence.

He kicked the shift into gear. "It won't happen again."

From the other side of the cab came only a long, drawn-out sigh.

Of frustration? Irritation? Regret?

Yeah, he felt the same.

If he'd been thinking straight, he'd never have taken things this far. Or gotten this close to actions he might never escape. Accidents happened, and he wanted nothing to do with the consequences that could result from them.

He jammed his foot on the gas pedal. With a roar of the engine and a tug on the steering wheel, he swung the truck around in the direction of town.

He'd fought hard during this damned long week to keep his mind on his goals. As if he didn't already have enough to deal with, his conscience would bother him now, for sure.

Should've listened to those instincts.

Should've kept those hands off her.

Should've realized you can't trust yourself around her.

TESS HURRIED to finish loading the dishwasher.

Simple exhaustion from all the stress had made her sleep like a rock that night. No dreams of Caleb. No nightmares.

But no escaping him at the breakfast table the next morning, either. She had struggled to survive the meal without staring at him as if she were some lovestruck teenager.

Like mother, like daughter.

She would have laughed at the irony of it—if her heart hadn't broken for her daughter's sake.

It was going to be a long day. The work party at Sam Robertson's ranch had expanded to include a barbecue afterward. And if that wasn't bad enough, just as they'd finished breakfast, Kayla called, asking her to bring Nate over early to keep Becky company.

Of course Tess had said yes, although agreeing had almost broken her. Now, more than ever, she needed to keep an eye on Caleb whenever he was with Nate. That would mean nearly all day and probably half the night at Sam's.

After breakfast, Caleb had disappeared without a word. Roselynn had left to drop Nate at Lissa's until they needed to leave for Sam's. Then she planned to pick up a few things at the store.

Finished loading the dishwasher, Tess hurried out to the yard to take down the laundry. She welcomed the chore to keep her mind occupied. She welcomed even more the chance to be alone.

In the hot sun, the bed linens had already dried. She folded as she went, dropping the items into her basket. As she took down the remaining sheet, she got a clear view of the opposite side of the yard. And what a view it was.

Caleb had just come around the corner of the shed. He'd

taken off his T-shirt, and she couldn't drag her gaze away. Her mouth went as bone-dry as the sheet in her hands.

That first night he'd stayed at the inn, she'd seen how good he looked standing half-undressed in the dim light of the hall outside his bedroom. Yesterday, in their encounter in the front seat of his truck—the encounter she'd since tried so hard to forget—she had touched all that goodness. Even through the fabric of his shirt, she'd felt hard muscle and heat.

Now he crossed the yard toward her. She shivered and clutched the sheet in her suddenly trembling hands—as if that would do any good. She'd be better off sitting on those hands to keep them out of temptation's way. And off temptation's six-pack abs.

Caleb closed in.

Walking—or running—away now would only make her look like a coward. Standing there shaking wouldn't give any better impression. She gathered up the sheet, crossed to one of the picnic benches and collapsed onto it.

Temptation came to a stop in front of her, looking hot— in more ways than one. Sexy, no doubt about that. And slightly sweaty, with his hair curled at the edges and a light film of moisture riding his tanned cheekbones. The urge to kiss that moisture away left her clutching the sheet so tightly, her fingers hurt.

To her dismay, he took the seat beside her. He sat backward on the bench and stretched his legs out in front of him. She saw him wince and had to swallow her murmur of sympathy.

As she glanced down, she saw what the hallway light *hadn't* shown her that night—a long, thin scar, sliced white against tanned skin, traveling up his rib cage and ending to one side of his chest in a sunburst of scar tissue.

This time she couldn't swallow her response. She

gasped and looked up to meet his eyes. "Caleb..." She couldn't finish. Didn't know how.

His shrug puckered the scarred skin even more. "That's nothing compared to the knee."

She licked her dry lips and fought to match his matter-of-fact tone. "They happened in the same accident?"

He narrowed his eyes, and she could read his question in them. She looked away, afraid to answer. No, she hadn't followed the news about him, or she would have known already. She wouldn't have asked him now.

After a moment, he said, "Yeah, the same time. That bull wasn't satisfied with throwing me off and stomping on my leg. He tried to run through me in a few places, too."

The statement made her lose any pretense of calm. Reaching out with her shaking hand, she traced the long, thin scar. "Does it hurt still?"

"Not right now, it doesn't." He half smiled, but she didn't need to see that to know what he meant.

"I'm sor—"

He lifted his hand and touched one finger to her lips. "Don't say it. I don't want that."

She moved her hand upward, sliding it to the patch of scar tissue. His heartbeat thrummed steadily beneath her palm. After a moment, she dropped her hand to her lap. But not before she'd felt his heartbeat pick up speed.

She sighed. "I wish I knew what you *did* want," she murmured, looking away. "You say you're here to buy property, but you don't seem interested in anything I've shown you so far. And then yesterday... Caleb," she said, unable to stop herself from blurting the thing that had bothered her most since then. The apology she'd never made. "When we were out in the desert and you'd talked about us, you said I knew I wasn't going to get anywhere with you."

She waited. He didn't respond, didn't look toward her, but she could tell by the way he sat, without moving a muscle, that he was listening to her.

"You said I knew it so well, that's why I didn't tell my family about you. And you thought it was because I pitied you. But I never have." She hung on to the sheet in her lap, needing to do something with her trembling hands. "I didn't keep our relationship from my family because of *you*. I did it because of me."

"You?" He still wouldn't look at her. "Why?"

She sighed. "Because my grandfather would have skinned me alive if he'd found out I was dating anyone."

At that, he turned his head, his eyes squinted in a frown. "You were seventeen."

"I know that. But he didn't think I should date anyone until I graduated. He was strict about it, almost obsessed over the idea of my focusing on my education. My mother dropped out of high school, and I think he thought I'd do the same." She shrugged. "It didn't matter. There wasn't anyone I wanted to go out with, anyhow. Until that day at the Double S."

Now she was the one who wouldn't make eye contact.

She and Dana had stopped in at the café after school for sweet teas. Football practice ended early, and Paul had shown up unexpectedly. The three of them shared a booth, but Paul made it so obvious he wanted to be alone with Dana that Tess couldn't help but catch on. Before she could speak up, could think of an excuse to leave, he had made the first move, and he and Dana had left her alone in the café.

"I was in pretty bad shape that day," she said, able to smile about it now. "It felt like Dana and I never had time alone together anymore. She was always somewhere with Paul. That was the first time in weeks we'd been able to hang out, just the two of us. Then they went off without me." She laughed. "It wasn't till they were gone that I discovered I didn't have enough money to pay for the sweet teas."

"I remember," he murmured.

"You saved me that day, giving me the change from your tips to make up the difference. If Granddad ever found out I'd tarnished his reputation by not paying what I owed, he would have grounded me till graduation."

"Dori and Manny would've let you slide."

"I didn't know that. But you were there for me. I never thanked you for that."

"I didn't hold it against you."

"No." But he'd held her against him not long ago, about as tightly as she now clutched the sheet. She dropped it to her lap and said, "Another thing about yesterday...when you said you'd gotten carried away..."

"And you won't hold that against me, will you?"

"You said it wouldn't happen again."

He leaned closer.

She stiffened, still not able to look at him. And now not daring to breathe.

"It won't happen," he said, his voice low. "Unless you want it to."

He stroked her jaw lightly with one finger.

Warmth spread up her neck into her cheeks. "I—"

"Oops. Well, excuse me!"

She jumped, startled by the unexpected interruption, though not at all surprised by whose voice she had heard. She turned away from Caleb to face her aunt.

"I didn't mean to interrupt."

"You're not," Tess said, rising from the bench.

Just as Caleb had saved her from an embarrassing situation that day in the Double S, Aunt El had saved her now—from giving in to temptation. From making yet another mistake. "I was just collecting the laundry, but I need to go over to my office for a while. Lots of paperwork to do before we go off for the rest of the day."

As she'd spoken, she had gathered up the sheet, crossed the yard again and grabbed the laundry basket.

Then she smiled at them both and fled.

TESS HAD FORGOTTEN about Roselynn borrowing the car.

She took her bag with the office keys in it and walked the few blocks to Wright Place Realty, hoping to burn up her nervous energy. She couldn't. And once at her desk, she had nothing to occupy her. So she simply paced the floor of the sunlit room and wondered how she'd managed to get herself into this predicament. And how she was going to get out of it in one piece and with her emotions intact.

Why couldn't she just have been satisfied with Joe Harley? Why couldn't she have accepted his proposal one of the many times he'd offered it? Then she wouldn't have had to face this dilemma at all.

But good old Joe didn't… Joe couldn't…

She sighed, forced to admit what she knew.

Joe wasn't who she wanted.

She'd been so foolish with Caleb just now, reminding them both of what had happened the night before.

The rush of excitement she'd felt when he'd held her proved how much she still cared about him. His kiss had only increased her desire to get closer. Whether she would have found the strength to push him away, she would never know.

He'd moved first, backing off in a rush. Admitting he'd gotten carried away. Assuring her that kiss would never happen again.

At the same time, she'd become obsessed by a wish that it would never end.

Again, she berated herself for mentioning anything to him.

So foolish. So naive. So completely idiotic.

How could she have left herself that vulnerable to him? And in front of Aunt El, too?

A sudden flash through the office window caught her attention. Outside, sunlight glinted off the windshield of Dana's van as she eased it to a stop at the curb.

Groaning, she dropped her head into her hands. They had spoken on the phone and exchanged emails but hadn't seen each other since the day at Ben's ranch.

She didn't want to see Dana now. How could she, when her best friend would take one look and know something was wrong? She would have to bluff her way through this. After a long, deep breath, she pasted a smile on her face.

The front door swung open.

Dana stood on the threshold and shook her head. "You'll give me a bad name with folks for making you come in on a Sunday."

"We can always claim work overflow."

"Ha." Dana closed the door and went to take a seat behind her desk.

Tess raised her brows in surprise. "What are you doing here?"

"I saw the lights on and thought maybe our landlord was up to something sneaky."

Tess laughed, sure that's what Dana had intended. "That's ridiculous. Squeaky-clean, boy-next-door Ben?"

"Just kidding. Actually, I didn't come in to discuss Ben. I saw you sitting here."

"Oh." Suddenly wary, she looked down at her desk and brushed an imaginary speck of lint from its surface.

"I'm as sure as I can get," Dana said, "you've got something you want to tell me."

Tess put her palms flat on the desk and breathed deeply again. After all these years, how could she confess to her closest friend? But how could she keep on the way she was now, holding back the truth from her?

And from Caleb?

A chilling wave of guilt rushed over her. Shivering, she pushed the thought aside. She couldn't tell him. Not now. Not ever.

But the time had come for her to confide in Dana.

"You're right," she admitted. "I do need to talk to you. About Caleb. He… I…." She could find no easy way to say this. "We went together senior year in high school. Just for a while, right before he left town."

"Yes, I know."

She almost choked on her indrawn breath. "You *what?* How? For how long?"

"Since high school." When Tess's mouth dropped open, Dana laughed. "And how? Come on—I was your best friend. I knew when you suddenly had no time to hang around after classes. And when you started leaving my house early on the weekends." She smiled and added gently, "And I saw the way you looked at him when we got to school every morning."

"You didn't. *I* didn't."

"Yes, you did."

"Oh, great." She slumped and ran her fingers through her hair. "Did everyone figure it out?"

"No, just me."

"Well, that's some consolation." She looked up. "I'm sorry I never told you, Dana. I couldn't let anyone know. If Granddad had ever found out…"

"You don't need to explain that. Why do you think I kept it to myself? So, now Caleb's here. And you are...?"

"In a mess. A real mess. I don't know why he had to come back again." She couldn't keep the bitterness from her tone. "He's not planning to stay, whether he buys property or not. Nate worships him, and he told her point-blank he doesn't belong in Flagman's Folly."

"And you haven't told him about Nate?"

"No, and I sure don't—" The blood drained from her face. She gripped the edge of the desk. "You know that, too?"

"I guessed. And just to make sure, I cornered Roselynn and Ellamae when I saw them at Ben's. Your mother confirmed it."

"She didn't!"

"Of course she did. Your aunt wouldn't budge when I asked. But you know your mother's nothing like Ellamae."

"*Nobody's* like Aunt El," she muttered, thinking of the campaign her aunt was running to reintroduce Caleb all over town. A sudden chill shot through her. How much had her aunt overheard earlier? How much had her own unwise decision hurt her?

She shook her head, forcing herself to stay on track. "Mom couldn't keep a secret if she— Oh..." She laughed weakly. "Of course she could, if she's known about Caleb all these years. Aunt El has to know, too. But how?"

"Not from me."

"Dana..." She hesitated. "I'm sorry I never told you about Nate, either."

Dana shrugged and looked away, making her feel worse than ever. "Everyone has secrets."

"I don't anymore. Not from you. But I haven't told Caleb anything." She still couldn't. How could she have let herself forget that long enough to get so close to him?

In as few words as she could, she shared the story of her long-ago trip to Gallup to find him, of how he had treated her, of how she had flung out the news about her marriage.

Of the way he'd wished her luck.

"What would I know about luck?" she asked scornfully. "If I'd understood it at all, I'd have known getting involved with him was the unluckiest thing that could have happened."

"But then Nate happened," Dana said softly.

Tears sprang to Tess's eyes. That was one thing—the only thing—she could never regret. "Yes, I have Nate. Thanks to Caleb. And," she added, her voice shaking, "I have to get him out of here before either of them finds out."

CALEB LOOKED AROUND the kitchen in amazement.

Roselynn had already cooked a mess of stuff to bring to Sam Robertson's that afternoon. And now she and Ellamae had started in cooking again. Far as he could tell, between them, they'd cleaned out the store. And still they'd forgotten a couple of things.

When Ellamae had left to go to Harley's, Roselynn came up with a long list of items she needed him to get down from the highest shelves in the pantry.

"I can't tell you how much I appreciate all you've done around here," she told him.

"My pleasure." He meant it. Especially this minute, when work could take his mind off the talk he'd had with Tess such a short while ago. And keep him from dwelling on how close he'd come to doing something he shouldn't have.

He'd worked up a sweat fixing the shed in the yard. Tess's hands on him had made him hotter. They'd been alone, the house deserted. He'd wanted to pick her up, sheet and all, and carry her inside. When he'd stroked her face, the look in her eyes told him he might just have gotten his wish. If Ellamae hadn't come along.

If Ellamae hadn't saved him from himself.

"Tess tries to help out," Roselynn said with a shrug. "But neither of us has money to burn."

He did. He'd just somehow gotten offtrack about his idea of setting it to flame. Gotten too hot over Tess to keep his thoughts and his hands where they belonged. And damn him for forgetting his plan to make Tess see what she'd walked away from. Instead, he'd started obsessing about everything *he* had missed.

He had to struggle to focus on her mama.

"And she's got so much on her mind with Nate."

"I noticed. A lot of friction between them." But anyone could tell they and Roselynn and Ellamae all loved each other. The way a family should.

Sighing, she reached for the baking dish he'd handed down from the stepladder. "You're right, those two are always at sixes and sevens. It's awful to see. You must think they don't care for one another at all."

He shook his head. "I'm certain it's the opposite. They just don't let it show often enough."

"That's so true." She set the next baking dish beside the first one. "I try to take on some of the responsibility with Nate, but you know Tess. She's always too hard on herself."

"Yes, she is." Too quiet, as well. "Must be a challenge having to raise the child on her own. With your help, of course."

She smiled. "I've tried to do what I could. It's not easy. Nate's a bit rebellious at times."

"I noticed that, too."

They both laughed, but he sobered quickly. Their talk

reminded him of that first day he'd come back, when Tess had told him her marriage hadn't worked out. Maybe it had fallen through before it even got started. He went with his hunch. "Tess never married at all, did she?"

"No, she never did." She hesitated, then said, "She didn't tell you about that herself?"

"Yes." He added grimly, "Though not in so many words."

"She's had plenty of chances." Roselynn sounded proud, the way a mama should sound when she talked about her kids. "Joe Harley's asked her more than once. But she's always said no. She's always put Nate first, you see. After you left, I think she felt—" She cut herself off and swallowed hard.

As if trying to take back her words? Too late. In these past few weeks, he'd already taken note of some things that didn't add up. She'd just given him another item for his list. "Why would you think my leaving had anything to do with Tess?"

"I didn't. I mean, I don't."

"And what's Nate got to do with this?"

"Nothing. Nothing at all. That was just me running my mouth again, as usual. If Ellamae hadn't left for the store already, she'd tell you so." She started fussing with the dishes on the counter.

He frowned. That first night he'd spent here and many times since, he'd seen how quickly she had left the dining room when the conversation made her uncomfortable.

The same way Tess had fled just a little while ago.

What was it Ellamae had said about Roselynn that night? That her sister "won't allow you much without a sugar coating on it." How much was she sweetening the truth now? He needed to know.

Stepping down from the ladder, he moved to stand in

front of her. "Roselynn," he said in the voice he'd use to calm a spooked mare, "what is it you're trying not to say?"

"I don't know what you mean." She kept her gaze on the baking dishes.

Between her innocent slip and her unwillingness to explain, he now had enough to figure things out—and he sure as hell didn't care for the total he'd come to.

"Roselynn," he said again, "is there something Tess won't tell me that I ought to know?"

"Please, Caleb," she said urgently, "don't ask me that." She scooped up both dishes, clanking them together. Finally, she met his eyes. "That's between the two of you."

Chapter Fourteen

"Don't worry, I'm turning off the lights," Tess reassured Dana as they prepared to leave the office. That done, she followed her friend outside and pulled the door closed behind them. "I don't want you to—"

Abruptly, she stopped.

At the curb behind Dana's van sat the rented pickup truck with Caleb at the wheel. And she thought she'd managed to escape him for a while.

"Here comes Nate." Dana pointed along Signal Street.

The three of them converged on the truck at the same time.

"All aboard for the Whistlestop," Caleb said.

Nate opened the passenger door and climbed in, moving to the seat in the rear of the cab. "C'mon, Mom."

Tess hesitated, not wanting to sit that close to Caleb again. And especially not wanting to get in that truck after what had happened between them in it.

Nate sat staring at her impatiently. Though Caleb's dark sunglasses hid his eyes, she could tell he watched her, too. Even Dana stepped back so that Tess could climb into the cab.

"Talk to you soon," Dana said.

As she nodded and climbed in, she gave thanks that this would be a quick and painless trip. Nate's chatter made the short ride go even more quickly. Still, she gave a sigh of relief when they reached the parking area of the inn.

Caleb opened the driver's door, and Nate jumped to the ground and ran toward the house.

When Tess reached for the passenger door handle, she was startled to feel his hand clasp her wrist. She looked at him in surprise. He released her arm, closed the driver's door and rested back against his seat.

"Let's compare notes," he said.

He could have chosen a better time than this. But she couldn't say that. She couldn't risk reminding him again of why they hadn't discussed the property last night. She grabbed her canvas bag from the seat beside her and began rummaging in it for her pen. "All right. Where do you want to start?"

"With Nate."

Her fingers closed convulsively on the notebook she'd just slid from the bag.

"You know," he continued, "the first day I met her, she told me she wasn't too happy with what you'd called her. 'Anastasia.' That's different. How'd you come up with it, anyhow?"

Her nails dug half-moon dents into the notebook's cover. She had to swallow hard before she could answer. She had to sound natural. Unconcerned. "I…looked it up in a baby-naming book. I thought it was pretty."

"And so it is. Goes nice with the rest of her name, too. 'Anastasia Lynn LaSalle.' You've called her that a couple of times when she's mouthed off to you. Of course, you didn't have to find that last one in a baby book, did you?"

"No, I didn't." She loosened her grip on the notebook but took a firmer hold on her emotions. Nothing to worry about here. He was only making conversation, more than likely prompted by Nate's chatter. "Now, what about that property we looked at just after lunch yesterday? The acreage is suited to what you need, and I'm sure we can get the asking price down. I've calculated—"

"Before we get into prices, let's calculate a few other things."

"Such as…"

"Years."

She frowned, puzzled. "For a mortgage?"

"For a marriage. Yours."

Her fingers convulsed again. If she gripped any tighter, she would risk a handful of ink when the pen broke in two. But there was no getting away from it. These weren't idle questions Caleb was asking. The confrontation she'd dreaded since the first day she'd seen him again had now begun. That didn't mean she'd go down without a fight. "What does my marriage have to do with anything?"

"A lot. Maybe more than I'd thought. You told me a while back it 'didn't work out.' How many years would it be if you were still married now?"

"That's none of your business."

"I'm calling you on that one, Tess. I think it *is* my business. You were never married at all."

"What makes you think that? Just because Nate has my maiden name? That doesn't mean a thing. Besides, whether I was married or not—or will marry Joe Harley or not—has nothing to do with you."

"Maybe not. But it's got something to do with Nate. And I should've seen that sooner. She's nine years old. I've been gone for ten. That's a simple enough calculation for me."

"Don't be so crude. Or so conceited." She forced a laugh. "I had plenty of time to—to find another boyfriend after you left."

"I'll give you crude, Tess. You teased me long enough

before you let me into your jeans. What are the chances you'd give away your favors to someone else only a couple months later?"

She gasped. Yes, his words had shocked her, as he'd planned. But worse, they'd hit the truth, too. She *wouldn't* have gone with someone else so soon after she'd given herself to him.

Nate came out of the back door and jumped down the steps, then headed in their direction. The huge grin on her face made Tess's heart hurt.

"Nate's mine, isn't she?" he demanded.

With shaking hands, she shoved her notebook and pen back into her bag. She had to get out of here.

He clasped her wrist again. "I'm not leaving this truck till you answer."

He would feel her tremors. Would see them. She couldn't help that. But as tears sprang to her eyes, she turned her head away. At least, she could keep him from seeing those.

Nate ran across the yard toward them.

Tess blinked furiously again. She couldn't let Nate see her this upset, either.

"Tess." He spoke her name gently. But relentlessly.

She slumped against her seat. Why did this conversation have to happen here? Why did it have to happen at all?

Nate was just a few yards away and coming closer, and still he pushed. "Tell me."

"Nate is not *yours,*" she burst out, her voice low but harsh with threatening tears. "She's ours." She reached blindly for the handle and yanked it, slid from the truck and slammed the door closed behind her.

"You coming in the house?" Nate asked.

"Yes." She'd go anywhere, do anything to avoid having

to be alone with Caleb again. From behind her, she heard the driver's door slam shut.

Surprising herself and Nate, she wrapped her arms around her daughter and squeezed tightly, wishing she would never have to let go.

To her shock, Nate returned the hug with equal enthusiasm.

CALEB STILL FELT THROWN by the news he'd learned.

Not discovering he was Nate's daddy. No, that was the best of it all.

After he'd left Roselynn, he'd walked around with his legs as shaky as the day he'd gotten out of his hospital bed to see if he could stand again. Maybe that's the way real daddies felt when they first saw their babies. He'd missed that step—and a few thousand others.

Thanks to Tess's deceit.

Her refusal to tell him about Nate only underscored the feelings he'd grown up with, the beliefs that had been reinforced in his time on the circuit. *Don't get too close to people.* He'd almost done that, almost trusted Tess. Almost shared his fears about having come so near to dying. Only to find she'd kept this secret from him all along.

Deep inside, he had to admit he understood that. At least, part of him did. He could see why she hadn't told him about the baby at first. That night in Gallup, he'd obsessed over winning his event, claiming his prize. Gaining the proof that showed how right he'd been to leave Flagman's Folly. And then wanting to show that proof to Tess. He'd sure messed that up.

Yet, another part of him didn't understand Tess's betrayal at all. That had been one night, one conversation. Since then, she'd had years to make another attempt to contact him, and still she'd kept the truth hidden. Even when he'd come back to town, she hadn't told him.

A while after he'd left Roselynn, he'd driven to Tess's office. Finding Nate and Dana there had put an end to any chance of talking to Tess alone. And when they'd gotten back to the inn, she had nearly run from the truck into the house.

Now he heard her footsteps in the hallway coming from the direction of her room. Easing his door ajar, he stood in the opening, waiting. No way would she get by him again, as she'd done downstairs, sticking close to Nate from the minute they'd come into the house so he wouldn't have a chance to talk with her alone. She'd come up here the same time as Nate, too, managing to cut him off again.

But she had run out of options for evading him.

Roselynn and Ellamae had never left the kitchen. Nate had gone into her room but had barreled down the stairs a few minutes ago. No one left up here but the two of them.

Her footsteps neared. He stood his ground, and when she saw him in the doorway, she froze.

He caught her gaze and held it long enough to send his message. Then he backed a couple of paces and swung the door open wider.

She sighed and waited.

So did he.

It could almost have been a replay of that first night he'd spent at the inn. Only now, a lot more had passed between them. A lot of empty words. *No one pitied you, Caleb. Not everyone thought less of you.* When he'd asked her if she'd felt that way, she had shaken her head.

Yet she'd kept his daughter from him.

She stepped into the room, closed the door and turned to face him. She had freshened up, pulling her hair back with some sparkly combs, putting color into her cheeks.

Adding something shiny to her lips that made them look softer than ever and ready for a kiss.

And damn him, he wanted to kiss her again.

She leaned back against the door, as if wanting as much distance between them as she could get. "Can we just let this go?"

Anger fired through him, making his hands shake. "I don't know," he said, proud of keeping his voice low. Not so proud of his struggle to drag his attention from her mouth. "You could try distracting me."

The flare of anticipation in her eyes almost crushed him.

She didn't want *him,* she just hoped to put off having this conversation. To avoid making the truth known to everyone.

Disgusted with himself, he moved over to the bureau and pawed through a drawer for a couple of bandannas. It would be hot working outside in the sun.

Not as hot as he felt inside this room.

In the mirror, he could see her staring at him. Could almost see her thoughts turning in her head. She might not want him, but he sure as hell felt the need for her—to make love or to settle a score, he couldn't tell right now. Just as well he'd never find out.

"No sense getting off course, is there?" he asked. "That's what brought us here today." He faced her again, opened his mouth, then shut it. Wincing inwardly, he thought of what she'd said to him in the truck earlier.

Don't be so crude.

He had the right to what he was going to say now. But he didn't have to be offensive about it. Despite everything, she had done a good job raising their daughter, with no help from him. He had to give her that.

That's all he'd allow.

"I'm going to talk with Nate."

"No." She surged forward, stumbled to a stop halfway across the room to him. "I won't let you do that."

"Let?"

She lifted her hands palm-up, then dropped them to her sides, but not soon enough for him to miss seeing she was the one shaking now. "All right. Then I'm asking you, Caleb. Don't do this."

Unable to stop himself, he laughed shortly. "Did you think I'd just walk away and forget what you told me?"

"No, I didn't expect you to forget. But walk away? Yes. Why wouldn't I think that? You've done it before."

"And you'll never let me off the hook for it."

She shoved her hand through the air, pushing his words away. "That's not what I meant. Not what we're talking about. It's Nate I'm thinking of. We can't just tell her this now and then go out for the day as if nothing had happened."

Being called crude, he'd accepted, but he'd be damned if he'd let her think him cruel and not defend himself. "What the hell makes you think I'd do that? Give me some credit, Tess. I won't tell her today. And I won't hit her point-blank with the news. You can pave the way for the conversation. But I'll be the one to tell her."

"What good will it do for you to talk to her? You're leaving again soon. She's never known about you. She doesn't need to know now."

"Who said that's for you to decide?"

"I'm her mother."

"And I'm her daddy."

"Yes," she shot back, "and it will be better for her if she never knows that."

The heat of her words slammed into him. She couldn't have made her feelings more plain, her rejection more final. He'd wanted the real reason behind her refusal to tell him about Nate even after all the years. Now he had it.

Even after she had said she'd never looked down on him.

He had to take a breath before he could respond. Before he could think at all. Still, her belief didn't make him any less determined.

He crossed the room, walking past her without looking, and threw open the door. "I'm telling Nate the news, Tess. When I do, you can be there for the conversation or not. Your choice."

CALEB DROVE the final nail into the wood and eyed Sam Robertson's new chicken coop with satisfaction. Amazing what a little hard labor could do for a man's aggressions.

All afternoon, he'd managed to act as though he hadn't a worry in the world.

The way Tess had kept up her lies for all these years. How hard had that been for her? And after the truth she'd kept from him, why should he care? Because she was the mother of his child?

The thought made him hot and cold at the same time. He swung the hammer again.

"Not bad for amateurs, huh?" Sam asked.

A few of his ranch hands had helped with the work, but they'd all taken off to shower, leaving the two of them to finish up.

Caleb dropped the hammer into the box with the other tools. "Looks like a pro job to me. Besides, I wouldn't call you an amateur. I saw that workshop of yours in the bunkhouse. And Dori told me you made the sign over the door at the Double S."

Sam shrugged. "Thanks." He finished rolling up the last of the tarps they'd used.

"I could do with a couple of those for next week," Caleb said. "I'm getting ready to do some painting over at the Whistlestop."

He'd already told Roselynn he'd do the work. Besides, he planned to stick around, no matter how Tess felt about him. No matter how much he wanted to walk away from her now. He wouldn't leave until he'd told Nate the truth.

"Help yourself," Sam said. "Let me know if you need a hand. I can send some of the boys over your way."

"That's not necessary. It's only one small room. It won't take much time."

Sam grinned. "Tess has you working, huh?"

"Roselynn does."

"Good thing. It'll keep you out of trouble."

"Maybe." More than likely, it would keep him in Roselynn's good graces, that was all. If she would still speak to him after she found out he'd confronted Tess.

Roselynn and Ellamae had been working hard in the kitchen when he'd left to drive over here with Nate. And with Tess, who hadn't said anything at all to him directly since she'd walked out of his room.

"Let me get us a refill." Sam went over to the insulated water cooler his wife, Kayla, and Tess had kept refilled.

Caleb stripped off his T-shirt and felt the pull of the scar tissue on his chest. Remembered the feel of Tess's hand as she'd touched him there.

He used the T-shirt to scrub the sweat from his face. Along with working off aggressions, the hot sun and hard labor made for good physical therapy. His knee hadn't given him much trouble at all. Too bad he couldn't say the same about his thoughts.

Despite everything, thinking of Tess while he'd worked had made him hot, bothered *and* troubled.

Catching sight of her across Sam's yard throughout the day hadn't helped, either. She wore a pair of jeans that fit her well enough to destroy his concentration—a dangerous thing for a man with a hammer in his hand. If that wasn't bad enough, she wore another blouse with an elastic neck that had him fixating on what had happened the day before.

He'd obsessed over that damned blouse all day yesterday, waiting for the chance to slide it off her shoulders and do just what he had done. He shook his head at the memory.

They had experienced some intense times as teenagers, but he'd never felt the way he had in that truck. Their talk had broken new ground, too, carrying them to the verge of a closeness they'd never arrived at years ago.

A closeness that could lead him into making promises he couldn't keep.

That morning, as he'd sat staring at her during breakfast, his mind had kept running through the whole list of reasons he didn't want to get involved with her.

Now he had to get involved. At least at some level.

Sam returned and handed him an oversize tumbler filled with cold water. He downed a gulp of it and settled back against the fence beside the coop. Across the yard, Tess and Kayla and Sam's mother worked at setting up for the barbecue. Folks would start showing up before too long.

On the back porch, Nate sat with Sam's five-year-old, Becky. Their hands waved in the air as they talked to each other in sign language.

"Looks like the girls get along," he offered.

Sam smiled. "They do. Nate's a good kid to spend so much time with a little one like Becky."

Nate *was* a good kid, despite her frequent shortness with her mama. He'd begun to care too much about both of them. At the same time, he couldn't stop thinking about how much he'd missed of Nate's life—thanks to Tess's lies.

Why was he wasting time over thoughts that would only tear him apart? In the long run, obsessing wouldn't change anything. He knew what he would do. His childhood here in town, his ten years in rodeo, his talk with Tess just the day before—they had all paved the way to his decision.

He tightened his grip on the T-shirt he'd stripped off, trying to stop thoughts of yesterday. They came to him, anyway.

Tess had wanted to know what knowledge he'd gained from being on the rodeo circuit. Chances were, his answer wouldn't have pleased her. He'd learned a lot. And of all the lessons the circuit had taught him, he thought again of the one he'd learned especially well: *No sense in forming personal ties. They don't last.*

For some people, anyhow. They seemed to have worked out fine for Sam Robertson. Caleb could hear the pride in the man's voice every time he talked about Becky.

He swallowed another gulp of water that seemed to clog in his throat. Clearing it, he said, "Tess told me Becky came to live with you not that long ago. That must have made some big changes in your life."

"It sure did." Sam looked across the yard at his wife and daughter.

The smile on his face made Caleb feel suddenly envious. On the one hand.

On the other hand, it made him want to bolt.

What did he know about being a daddy?

"I guess you've gone through a few changes lately, too," Sam said.

Caleb frowned. Then he realized Sam must have meant his rodeo career. "Been a crazy time," he agreed. He paused, then went on, "Judge Baylor told me about you two coming to the hospital."

"Yeah. The news stories had started to slow down. Folks wanted an update on how you were doing."

"I wouldn't think they'd send a posse as far as Dallas to find out."

"We figured firsthand was the only way we'd get information. We'd have gone clear to the East Coast, if we'd needed to. Trust me on that." Sam picked up the water cooler. "I'd better go check the barbecue before I hit the shower."

Caleb nodded and watched the other man walk away.

Somehow, he did trust Sam Robertson. They hadn't run into each other much when he lived in town, but when they did, the man had always been decent.

Sam said folks had cared when he'd had the accident. A big concept to wrap his head around. Growing up, hardly anyone had bothered about him. Yet, since his return, all the townsfolk had shown him interest and concern.

Sam said pretty much the same things the judge had said.

Did that mean he had to trust the judge's words, too? About everything?

He unclamped his fingers from his T-shirt and tossed it onto one shoulder. Slowly, he smiled. That chip Judge Baylor claimed he carried around had just started to slide out of place.

Then he glanced across the yard again and felt his smile slide out of place, too.

Since his return, all he'd gotten from Tess was the feeling she wanted him gone. Or was it?

In the truck yesterday, he'd taken it upon himself to back off, out of respect for her. Before he'd done that, though, she had started warming up in a way he sure liked.

She'd seemed willing enough to get close to him that morning, too. At least till Ellamae had shown up.

He looked over toward the trestle tables in the yard.

Tess's face lit as she listened to something Kayla told Sam. Her cheeks flushed pink from sunshine or laughter or her movements as she leaned down to smooth a cloth over the tabletop. Even from here, he could see a sparkle in her eyes.

What would've happened if he hadn't backed off yesterday?

And why the hell was he thinking about it?

After that confrontation in his bedroom, nothing could happen between them now.

Chapter Fifteen

Tess looked over toward the porch, where Nate and Becky carried on their play, half in sign language and half in the way they moved Becky's toys through a dollhouse Sam had made for her.

Her puppy, Pirate, lay flat on his belly beside them.

Every time they saw Becky, she and Nate picked up a few more signs. And Nate always enjoyed the little girl's company. Still, knowing her tomboy daughter would much prefer to muck out the stalls in Sam's barn than play with dolls, Tess couldn't help but smile. Nate looked up, caught her gaze and smiled back.

Tess blinked rapidly, fighting off a wave of tears.

Prickly, exasperating and *belligerent.* No one with any sense could deny those words applied to Nate. *Precious, loving* and *beloved* did, too. How was she going to react when Caleb told her the news?

Tess braced her hands on the picnic table. Hurt and humiliation washed over her. She had sworn Caleb would never know about their child. Too late for that now.

Resignation flooded through her, too. Much as she didn't want to admit it, she'd made the choice years ago to hold back from Caleb something he had the right to know. Now he'd found out. Now she had no choice. She had to accept his need to tell Nate the truth.

He strode across the yard toward Tess, as if he'd heard her thought and planned to act on it that very moment. Even as a cold sweat broke over her, she told herself it couldn't be true. He wouldn't talk to Nate here.

As he approached, she stared. He was shirtless again now, and the memory of touching him made her fingers tremble just as they had that morning.

She wanted to touch him again.

Her cheeks burning, she grabbed the pile of napkins Kayla had left on the table. Napkins now, sheets and pillowcases earlier today. None of them could occupy her hands well enough.

She looked over her shoulder, but Sam, who might have provided some interference, had just entered the bunkhouse. Kayla had followed his mother into the house. Even Nate and Becky had left the porch swing and were rushing toward the barn, Pirate bounding at their heels. Everyone had deserted her.

She tried to swallow, but her throat wouldn't cooperate. Tried to rise, but her legs wouldn't obey her.

Then she got a grip on her napkin—and on her emotions. If she couldn't be strong for herself, she'd damned well better practice being strong for her daughter.

Just as Caleb neared her, she heard the sound of a car on Sam's gravel drive. The familiar chugging noise of its engine made her sag in relief. She'd fight Caleb for what she had to. But not here. Not now.

Tess rose, and they both started toward the Toyota, where Roselynn and Aunt El had begun unloading the backseat. They seemed to have brought enough to feed the crowd on their own.

"Let me take some of that off your hands," Caleb offered.

Aunt El looked at her, then eyed him up and down, her

gaze lingering on the T-shirt that only partially hid his bare chest. "Seems like you might have enough on *your* hands already."

Tess felt her cheeks burn. What did she think the two of them had been up to? Then again, how much had she seen this morning? Sighing, Tess said, "Never mind, Caleb. You need to go shower. I'll take care of these two."

He shrugged, then nodded and headed in the direction of the bunkhouse.

"Hey, Caleb," Ellamae said, "need someone to scrub your back?"

He pivoted, his face split in a grin. "Why, thanks, ma'am, but I wouldn't want to put you out."

She laughed. "Don't be silly. I wasn't offering to do it myself." She looked at Tess.

Shaking his head, he turned away.

Shaking with fury, Tess turned on her aunt, but pent-up emotion made the words catch in her throat. The tension with Nate. The angry confrontation with Caleb. The years she'd spent keeping a secret that wasn't a secret from those closest to her at all. Finally, she found her voice. "Aunt El. Mom. What is it you two are trying to do?"

"Help you, sugar," Roselynn said.

"Like always," Aunt El added gruffly.

"Oh-h." The word threatened to become a wail. Tess swallowed hard, her eyes misting. "I know you've always meant well," she began. "I just didn't realize how much, until today. Dana told me you both know…everything about me and Caleb."

"I heard tell you were out walking with him a few times," Ellamae said.

"'Heard tell'?" Tess shook her head. She could laugh about it now. Sort of. "What you mean is, you sicced your spies on me."

Her aunt shrugged. "Whatever it takes."

"We were worried about you."

"I know you were, Mom. You, too, Aunt El." Tess reached out and gave them each a quick hug. "Thank you. I appreciate it more than I'll ever be able to say. But I'm a big girl. You've got to let me act like one. Let me take care of this myself, all right?"

"Hey, Gram!" Nate shouted from the barn doorway.

She and Becky ran up to them, followed by Pirate.

"Gram, did you bring the chocolate pie?"

"We sure did," Roselynn said. "And we've got to get it into the house."

"Along with the rest of this food. Here, Tess."

Aunt El shoved the foil-covered casserole into her hands and proceeded to lead the way to Sam's back porch.

It wasn't till much later that Tess realized neither her aunt nor her mother had made any promises about letting her take care of her problems on her own.

HOURS LATER, Caleb would eagerly have swapped the back scrub he didn't get for the back massage he now needed. Though on second thought, he could have fared worse if Tess had taken up Ellamae's suggestion. He still couldn't hold back an unwilling smile every time he recalled the look on Tess's face when she'd heard what her aunt had said.

He put both hands to his lower back and stood straighter, trying not to look like he hurt as much as he did. So much for his hard labor being good therapy. He hadn't finished his shower yet before the aches had set in.

"Grab yourself a chair before they're all gone," Ben Sawyer advised him.

"Don't mind if I do," he said.

He took one of the lawn chairs Ben offered him and

sat in it. With a sigh, he stretched his feet out toward the fire they'd just started in a cleared ring well away from Sam's house and barn. And the brand-new chicken coop that didn't look half bad at all.

"Did that big supper do you in?" Ben asked.

"That and the games," he confessed. He wasn't about to mention the coop, which had started it all.

After the barbecue and a few rounds of horseshoes—in which Judge Baylor whupped most everyone's butt—he felt more than ready to take a break. The need for the rest bothered him, but there it was. He would never be the same man he'd been a couple of years ago.

Did it matter much, when that man might not have been the person he'd always thought, anyhow? Folks like the judge and Sam and even Tess, he admitted reluctantly, were making him change his perceptions about himself. And about the past.

On the opposite side of the ring, Tess had just taken a vacant chair. She sat staring at the fire, her eyes glowing from the reflected flames.

They hadn't had another chance that day to be alone. Much better that way.

"Hey, Caleb, can we sit with you?" Nate asked.

"Sure," he said.

Today, same as at Ben's potluck, Nate had gotten too involved playing games with her friends to pay much attention to him. Come to think of it, their tendency to hang around had slacked off lately, too. As if the girls had started to get used to seeing him. As if they, in agreement with Ben's statement about the townsfolk, took for granted he belonged.

The thoughts left him with a funny feeling beneath the scarred skin of his chest.

Nate and Lissa and Becky squeezed their way between

his chair and Ben's. Becky's pup hovered behind them, his tail wagging. Ben shifted his chair to give them more room, and Caleb did the same.

"Thanks." Nate plopped onto the ground next to him.

Her friends took places beside her. Pirate dropped to his haunches and rested one paw on Becky's knee.

The girls unfolded a game board and started to divvy up cards.

A burst of laughter broke out from one point in the circle of chairs around the fire ring. Voices rose left and right as more people pulled up chairs.

Caleb sat back and recalled the questions that had taken over his thoughts more often than they should have today.

What if he and Tess hadn't split up permanently? Would they have lasted till now?

He looked down at Nate's dark head. If he and Tess had gotten back together, they could have raised Nate with both a mama and a daddy. Might have had a few other kids along the way.

But they hadn't, thanks to Tess.

Like a flame in the fire ring, a flare shot up inside him. He had to get beyond that thinking. What had happened— or not happened—couldn't matter anymore. He had to look forward, keep his eye on the future.

Do right by his child.

He couldn't follow what his own mother had done. Ignored him. Virtually abandoned him. Left him wondering about his daddy.

He clutched the metal armrest of his chair and swallowed the bitterness that rose to his throat. Yes, in another way, he had deserted Tess by turning from her years ago. But he'd never known about their baby. He did now.

He wouldn't let his daughter think he'd abandoned her.

At that moment, Nate looked away from her game and

up at him. Her eyebrows wrinkled in a frown. Grasping the arm of his chair, she leaned toward him. "What's the matter, Caleb?"

"Not a thing," he said. "I'm just sitting back and enjoying myself."

She leaned closer and whispered, "Then why do you look so sad?"

ALL THROUGH BREAKFAST, Tess's stomach churned. She couldn't touch her eggs, could only pretend to sip her tea.

Last night, Caleb had insisted he would talk to Nate this morning.

Tess had spent a long time after that closeted in the kitchen with her mom and then an even longer night awake in her room.

The three adults had eaten little. They said even less.

Nate picked up on the tension.

By the time Roselynn had gone into the kitchen, closing the door firmly behind her, Nate looked apprehensive. When Tess asked her to come into the living room, her expression froze. She looked over at Caleb.

"You comin', too?"

"Wouldn't miss it."

In the living room, feeling suddenly chilled, Tess grabbed the crocheted afghan from the couch and crossed to the rocker in one corner. She took her seat and clutched the afghan in her lap. Somehow, she had to start this conversation that would change all their lives forever. At least Caleb had given her the chance to make the news easier for Nate to hear.

He sat on the couch and leaned forward, resting his elbows on his knees and linking his fingers together in front of him.

Nate plopped onto the leather ottoman. "I'm in big trouble, right?"

"Of course—"

"No, you're—"

Tess and Caleb each cut themselves off.

Not looking at him, she said, "You're not in any trouble, Nate. Why do you think that?"

"I just do." She scuffed her sneaker on the braided rug beside the ottoman and added in a rush, "Aunt El said I'd get in hot water soon for mouthing off."

Tess couldn't help wondering if Aunt El ever thought about just where Nate got her sass. She smiled gently. "It's true, we could have less of that all around."

"I'm trying not to," Nate mumbled. "It's not easy."

"I know." She paused. Caleb sat watching them intently. If ever she had an opening to show him how well she could handle Nate—and how little she needed his interference in their lives—this was it. "I didn't mean just you, honey. I imagine I could snap a little less often, too."

"Yeah. That would be good."

Caleb met her eyes briefly, and her sudden contentment at the sense of a moment shared gave way just as quickly to a feeling of dismay. Sharing a moment with him had gotten her into more hot water than she could believe. With shaking hands, she clutched the afghan again.

"Nate, Caleb and I wanted to talk to you together."

Her daughter's eyes immediately sought his. He gave her a smile that made Tess's eyes mist.

Oblivious to her, Nate grinned back at him. "You feel better now? You're not sad anymore?"

Tess frowned. What was that about?

He shook his head. "No, as a matter of fact, I'd say I'm feeling pretty darned happy."

"Then, you mean," Nate said slowly, "you're going back to the rodeo?"

Tess almost sighed aloud at the irony of those words. No, Caleb would never go back to the rodeo circuit. But he *would* leave again. That's why she had fought with him about not telling Nate the truth. He'd left *her* once and she'd gotten over it. Eventually. But what would happen when he repeated history with their daughter? Would he break Nate's heart, too, when he left town?

"No, I'm not going back to rodeo, Nate."

"Oh, wow." She bounced on the ottoman. "Then you're staying here, right? I knew you would! Boy, wait'll I tell the guys."

"It'd be nice to stay, Nate." He looked down at his linked fingers. "But I can't do that permanently."

"Oh."

Tess took a deep breath. "Nate," she began, "you know that Caleb grew up here in Flagman's Folly."

"Yeah. That's why he came back."

"That's part of it, yes. But there's more. He also has something to share with you about when he lived here." She stopped and looked over at him.

He cleared his throat and took up the story. "When your mama and I were teenagers, we went together."

"Went where?" Nate asked.

"Uh, we went to high school together. And then we dated each other for a bit. You know what I mean?"

"Yeah." She nodded emphatically. "Like, boyfriends and girlfriends."

"Right. And then…" He faltered.

"And then you missed Mom and then you came back, and now you're gonna get married! I knew it."

"Nate—"

Before Tess could finish, she interrupted. "Wait a minute. You said you're not staying here." She frowned. "Then how are you gonna marry Mom?"

Tess watched as Caleb's fingers tightened, clamping his hands together.

"I'm not going to do that, either."

"You're not?" Nate spoke in a dull tone now, her eyes downcast. "Then you're just…leaving?"

Tess inhaled sharply and blinked back the moisture suddenly blurring her vision. This was ten years ago, all over again. Ten years ago, but much worse.

"No, I'm not leaving yet." He shifted to the edge of the couch and took a deep breath, as well. "Nate, I know this'll come as a surprise to you. A good one, I hope. What…your mama and I want to tell you is that…I'm your daddy."

Nate's head snapped up. Her eyes opened wide. Her jaw dropped. A bright red flush filled her face. "You are not! You're Caleb Cantrell."

"Nate," Tess said softly.

"Listen—" Caleb said.

"No, I won't listen!" Nate jumped up from the ottoman, her eyes glistening. "Don't let him say that, Mom." Her voice broke. She backed away. "You're a rodeo star. You can't be my daddy. You *can't*."

Before Caleb or Tess could say anything more, she turned and ran from the room.

They heard the sound of her sneakers slapping on the bare entryway floor, the front door opening, the metal screened door banging against its frame.

And then silence.

An uncomfortable, agonizing silence that lasted forever.

Caleb broke it, finally, by clearing his throat. He said nothing, only moved his hands in a groping, almost helpless gesture. She could envision him on the back of a horse or astride a bull, holding on to reins or grasping a saddle horn, fully in control.

Caleb was never helpless. Until his accident.

And until now.

She dug her fingers into the afghan in her lap, knowing she had to keep quiet for her own sake and for Nate's.

The look on his face and the hurt in his eyes wouldn't let her. But how did she find the words?

"It… This was a shock to her. You had to know it would be. You'll need to give her some time." She took a deep breath, bracing herself, knowing the only thing she could think of to help him was guaranteed to hurt her. "Nate's a preteen with a crush on you, Caleb. A girl who thinks she's in love. At some level, though, she realizes that's just a dream." She swallowed hard. "Believing you would…we might marry gave her a way to hold on to you. And now, she doesn't have that, either. All she's left with is the feeling she's humiliated herself."

He stared at her.

She stared back, unable to look away. Her pulse pounded at her temples. Her eyes felt tight from her effort to hold back tears.

Finally, he nodded slowly. "Yeah, I reckon you're right."

Chapter Sixteen

Tess stood outside Nate's bedroom door.

When she hadn't returned after a short while, Tess had tried not to panic. When an hour had passed with still no sign, she'd given up and called Dana. It seemed Nate had run directly to Lissa's house.

After Nate had arrived home, only to run right upstairs, Tess gave her a few minutes alone. And allowed herself a few minutes to compose herself before following.

Nate sat on her bed, leaning against the headboard, with her arms crossed over her chest. Her gaze rested on the poster of Caleb that now lay in a torn, tangled heap on the floor.

When she saw Tess looking at the poster, she muttered, "He's not my daddy."

Tess sat carefully on the side of the bed and put her hand on Nate's knee. "Honey, I'm sorry I never told you, but what Caleb said is true."

"How?"

With her free hand, she gripped the edge of the mattress. This was not the talk she'd planned to have right now. But she owed Nate an answer. "Well…we read that book together, remember?" she said. "The one about babies—"

"Not the babies," Nate said, anger blending with scorn.

She refused to look up. "I know all about that and how the boy's whatchamcallit—"

Good thing she wasn't watching Tess, who couldn't help staring in surprise. She didn't recall the book going into that much detail. "'Whatchamacallit?'"

"I can't remember the word. You know—the boy's swimming thing hits the girl's egg—and wham! There's a baby."

Tess opened her mouth and closed it again.

Nate continued, "The eighth-grade girls are always going on about that stuff in the cafeteria. But I'm not talking about that." Nate tilted her head down farther, her dark hair hiding her face. She hesitated, then went on in a softer tone. "I never saw Caleb. Except at the rodeo, I mean. And on posters. If he's my daddy, why wasn't he here before?"

Tess shook her head. Trust Nate to ask the tough questions. Before she could decide how to respond, Nate looked up.

Her expression made Tess's breath catch. Her tomboy daughter's eyes filled with tears.

"Didn't he even want me?" Nate's voice shook. Tears spilled over and ran down her cheeks. She scrubbed them away with the backs of her hands.

"Oh, honey." Tess reached for her.

As Nate sobbed against her, Tess held her close and kissed her hair.

CALEB LOOKED AROUND the breakfast table, where they all sat quietly, thinking their own thoughts.

In the couple of days since he'd learned he had a daughter, his life had changed. And not for the good, it seemed.

The morning he and Tess had talked to Nate, she'd disappeared afterward in a halfhearted attempt to run away from home that had ended by suppertime. Since then, she'd made sure their paths only crossed during meals, when she would sit scrutinizing him every time she felt sure he wasn't noticing.

Roselynn tried hard to keep things normal, yet the expression of pity he saw every time he caught her off guard didn't help much.

And Tess...

As clearly as if she'd put it on paper, Tess had drawn a parallel between the way she and Nate felt about him.

She'd drawn battle lines now, too. Their interactions remained all business, all the time, but even with that, she had trouble looking him in the eye.

He should have known better, about Nate. About Tess.

As luck would have it, she had found some nearby available acreage, a ranch that sat closer to the outskirts of Flagman's Folly than anything she'd shown him yet.

Another change he couldn't put on the good side of his life.

His grand plan for returning to Flagman's Folly had fallen as flat as the paper-thin crepes Roselynn had just served him. Sure, he'd come back to town knowing he was down and out of rodeo for good. But he'd gone out on top, dammit—and he'd wanted to show them all. Wanted to rub their noses in the proof of his success. Hard to do, though, when no one cared about those things but him.

With the way things stood, he couldn't deny Tess her commission. Well, he'd put all those rodeo winnings he'd saved up to good use and just buy the danged ranch.

"The property has about everything on your wish list," she said, her attention focused on her plate. "And it's ready for immediate purchase."

Nate's head shot up. She looked from Tess to him and back again.

"A stroke of good fortune," he said, "finding that property available right now."

"Yes," Tess said.

Nate's fork hit her plate so hard, the clank echoed in the suddenly quiet room. "Does that mean he's leaving soon?" she demanded, looking at Tess.

He tried not to wince at her eagerness to have him gone. How could he expect anything otherwise?

"Yes, that's what it means," Tess said.

She sounded relieved about it. He should have known that prying the truth from her and sharing it with Nate wouldn't make a difference to either of them.

"He's leaving 'cause of you, Mom!" Nate burst out.

Now he heard anguish in her tone. The realization forced him back in his seat in astonishment. Maybe he'd read her wrong.

She raised that strong jaw the way she had the first time he'd seen her, talking to her mama at the Double S, in the way that made her look so much like Tess. "You told him he was making comp—complications for everybody."

"Nate," Roselynn said hurriedly, "I'm sure that's not true."

"Yes, it is, Gram. I was in the hallway and I listened to them talking."

Tess sighed. "You know you shouldn't—"

"I *have* to listen! If I don't, nobody tells me anything. Like, about my daddy." She held such a grip on her fork, her knuckles turned pure white.

Tess's face paled to nearly the same shade. "Nate—"

"Everything's your fault!"

"Hold it," Caleb said. He couldn't let Tess take the brunt of Nate's anger. Now it *was* his place to speak up. "That's no way to talk to your mama. Let's try an apology."

The look Tess gave him would have made a better man turn tail and run.

Roselynn, about to reach for a platter, sat back empty-handed.

Nate looked from him to Tess. Carefully, she set her fork on her plate. "I'm sorry. May I be excused?"

"Yes, you may," Tess said.

"From the table," he added. "If you ask me, Nate, your bad manners are another story."

For a second, he'd have sworn her dark eyes shone with tears. Then she blinked and the image disappeared. "You sound just like Mom."

No one said a word as she shoved her chair backward, the legs screeching against the wood floor. She stood and pushed the chair up to the table, then looked at him again.

He waited for her to raise her jaw. She didn't. His hopes took a sudden leap. Maybe sounding like her mama had earned him a mark on the good side of his tally.

"I'm sorry for my bad manners, too," she said.

He nodded and tried a half smile. "Glad to hear it."

She smiled slightly in return. After taking one last, quick look at her mama, she turned away from the table.

"Don't go off too far, sugar," Roselynn said. "We promised Becky we'd bring over those books of yours, remember? Just give me a bit to get the dishes cleared up."

Tess rose and took the platter from Roselynn's hand. "You two go ahead. Caleb and I will take care of things."

He raised his brows. Helping with repairs around here didn't bother him. But when had he gotten nominated to do housework?

"Are you sure?" Roselynn asked.

Tess nodded, her mouth set in a grim line. "Oh, I'm sure. We've got a lot to clear up. Besides dishes." She grabbed a serving bowl, too, and stalked out of the room.

Roselynn sat wearing her pitying expression again.

"Oh, boy," Nate mumbled, her eyes wide. "Maybe you shoulda asked to be excused, too."

THE IMAGE of Caleb sitting at the table smiling at Nate, of Nate smiling back at him, had filled Tess with dismay. But now, as she rinsed dishes in the kitchen sink, her hands shook from a very different reason.

After Roselynn and Nate had left the house a short while ago, she'd gone into the dining room to continue clearing the table, only to discover Caleb had conveniently disappeared, too. If he thought his absence from the kitchen would save him, he'd have to think again.

She couldn't understand what had led her to behave the way she had these past couple of days. She had given in to his determination to tell Nate the truth. She had felt compassion when she'd seen how much Nate's rejection had hurt him. And she had kept up appearances as well as she could since then, even though she'd wanted to do nothing but take Nate and run with her as far away as she could.

But now this!

The way he'd stepped between her and Nate enraged her. All through these weeks, he'd seen how rebellious Nate was, how hard to handle at times. Didn't he know what his involvement would do to Nate? It would only confuse her. Only make it more difficult for her to understand after he'd left her.

After he'd left them both.

Behind her, she heard heavy bootsteps on the kitchen floor. She whirled from the sink, heedless of the water she'd sprayed across the counter, and faced him.

"How could you do that?" she demanded.

"What?"

Gritting her teeth, she grabbed a dish towel to dry her

hands. "Don't give me that. You know what. How could you discipline my daughter in front of me? What makes you think you have that right?"

"I'm her daddy."

"No, you are not. Not in the ways that count." To her horror, her voice broke. She clenched her fists and pushed on. "You haven't been her daddy from day one."

"And whose fault is that?" He crossed the kitchen and snatched the dish towel from her hands, slammed it down on the counter. "Quit worrying that damn towel, Tess, or you'll have it in shreds. And start making some sense. You never gave me a chance to be Nate's daddy. You never even told me you were pregnant."

"I tried to tell you. When I found you outside Gallup. That day I had to track you down." Suddenly, she realized her anger was less about his interference with their daughter and more about his indifference to her. About the way he'd tossed her aside. But she couldn't seem to stop her words, to keep the bitterness from her voice. Or the images from her mind.

"You don't remember anything about that day, do you?" she demanded. "How you were so eager to leave your one-horse town and the one-horse people in it. So eager to run into that arena to claim your trophy. Or your new belt buckle." Tears blurred her vision, threatening to spill. "Whatever it was, you got it. I just hope it was worth what you gave up."

She attempted to rush past him, but he reached out, catching her around the waist and turning her to face him. Her chest heaved with her ragged breaths as she fought for control. She could see him breathing unsteadily, too. Could see his eyes light with an emotion she couldn't name.

"Yeah, I remember," he said, his voice low. "I acted

like a jackass. But that's not what all this is about, is it?" he demanded. "I said it to you the first night I came back here. You'll never let me off the hook for leaving."

"Well, all right," she cried, reaching down, intending to push his arm away, "give the man a prize."

"I'll take it," he said.

She froze, confused. "What are you talking about?"

"You just offered me a prize. And I know what I want."

Her hand clamped involuntarily on his forearm. Her heart beat faster.

"You said it yourself, I'm leaving soon." He tucked his finger under her chin and with gentle pressure tipped her face up to his. He leaned down, leaving her no choice but to make eye contact with him.

In truth, she couldn't have looked away.

He waited the space of several heartbeats, then to her shock, he dropped his hand and stepped back.

Her hand fell to her side. Her heart raced. The pulse in her neck thudded against her skin. She'd barely regained control of her breath and he'd stolen it away again.

"Before I leave here, I want what you had for ten years and never gave me," he said, everything—his eyes, his face, his tone—hard and uncompromising. "I want time with Nate."

He turned and walked out of the kitchen without a backward glance, as if aware of how thoroughly he'd unsettled her. As if certain she wouldn't say a word.

As if knowing she couldn't refuse him.

She reached unseeingly toward a chair at the table and dropped into it.

He had forced the issue with Nate, and the damage had been done. If her daughter were an infant, a toddler, too young to understand, the situation would be different.

She could get away with telling Caleb to leave and never come back.

But Nate was a rebellious preteen with a mind and a will of her own. And she now knew Caleb was her daddy.

Tess gulped a mouthful of air, exhaled it on a long, shaky breath. No, she couldn't refuse Caleb. She wouldn't be able to live with herself if she forced him to walk away and break her daughter's heart.

The question was, would she be able to protect her own heart when he finally went off on his own again?

These past weeks had taught her another truth she wanted to ignore. That kiss they'd shared in his truck had opened her eyes to the possibility. Her compassion for him in the face of Nate's rejection reinforced the feeling. And the way she'd responded just moments ago, when she thought he was going to kiss her, turned that feeling into fact.

If the time had come for telling truths, she had to be honest about it. Finally. Not with him. She could never share it with Caleb. But she couldn't keep lying to herself.

She'd never gotten over him.

Worse, that kiss, that compassion, that moment of breathless anticipation, the yearning she couldn't deny— they all made her hope that, despite everything, Caleb's determination to get to know their daughter would bring them together again, too.

Chapter Seventeen

Caleb stretched his bad leg sideways on the porch swing and looked over at Nate, who'd already settled into roughly the same position on the top porch step.

Another week had passed. Phone calls from Montana made him feel pressured to get back home. Still, he stayed. He had important business here, too.

He'd tried to prepare Nate for his leaving, but she hadn't taken it well. He couldn't walk out on her right away.

Just yesterday, he and Tess had taken care of the paperwork for the property he'd agreed to buy. Knowing how much she and Dana needed the income, he couldn't resent the purchase. And he would find some way of making the investment pay off.

A good part of his time, he'd helped out with repairs around the inn and painting that room Roselynn needed done.

As the week had gone by, he'd continued to stop in often at the Double S to visit with Dori and Manny. He'd kept in touch with Sam and Ben and with others in town, too. It felt good to know he could talk to them all without that chip on his shoulder.

Resentment weighed him down only when he talked to Tess.

Along with their business discussions, they'd managed

to have a few amicable conversations. Somehow, he'd handled the constant temptation to touch her without giving in. But he'd started getting cramps in his fingers from clenching them into fists when she came anywhere close to him.

Better to keep from spending time alone with her, to have Roselynn and Nate around—and Ellamae, when she dropped in. Safety in numbers.

He wouldn't have to worry about that tonight. Tess had just gone upstairs to get ready for another date with good old Joe. The best thing, all around.

He looked over at Nate again. They'd made peace on Signal Street during the Fourth of July parade. For the price of a double-dip ice-cream cone.

Well, a sort of peace, and probably as close as they could have come then. But he continued to work at it and had felt gratified to see he'd made real progress.

Every day, he managed some time alone with her. Nothing special, just having her help while he made his repairs. Playing cards and checkers after supper. Relaxing with her outside, where he took his usual seat here on the swing and she settled onto her favorite spot on the step.

"You want grape or lime?" she asked, holding up a couple of wrapped candies.

"Lime." He pretended not to notice her relief. He'd already figured out she liked the grape-flavored best.

She got up to give him his candy, then returned to her seat. "Gram sure has lots of stuff for you to do around here."

He nodded. "She sure does. Good thing I have a great assistant."

She gave him a smile. She hadn't warmed up to him enough to reach her previous level yet. Maybe she never would. Fine by him—he didn't want the hero worship, the adoration, the crush. What he did want…he had no right to expect.

Plenty of times, he'd found her eyeing him as if she'd been trying to figure out what made him tick. She sat watching him that way now. He waited, knowing that sooner or later she'd come out with whatever she had on her mind.

This porch was the place they did most of their talking.

And the place he did a lot of his thinking whenever he found time hanging heavy. He tried not to let that happen often. Didn't want to risk getting too deep into his troubled thoughts.

"Before," Nate said suddenly, "did you ever wish you had kids?"

He froze in the act of rubbing his knee. She hadn't called him by name since the day he'd told her he was her daddy. But she'd asked a slew of intense questions about his relationship with her mama, his life on the circuit, and what he'd done since he couldn't ride.

With all those questions this week, she'd never brought up anything like this. He knew where she had to be headed.

"You know," he said, "I never did wish for kids, Nate. Never thought I'd have a family." Never wanted one. But he couldn't be that blunt.

That night around the fire ring at Sam's place, when she had asked him why he looked so sad, he hadn't known what to say. So he'd come up with something else. In all the time he'd thought about it since, he still didn't know how he'd find the right words.

He couldn't tell a nine-year-old anything he'd thought about while sitting in front of that fire. How his own mama had told him straight out he was nothing but a burden to her. Nothing but deadweight dragging her down.

That's the kind of family he knew about.

He couldn't give her an honest answer about that. He didn't want to talk about his past at all with Nate. With anyone. Yet with the truth he'd revealed to her just a week or so ago, how could he not tell her something about his life, too?

"Growing up," he began slowly, "I didn't have much of a family."

"You didn't?"

"No. No brothers or sisters. No cousins."

"Like me."

He nodded. He'd had no father, either. Like her, too.

Tess had shown him a photo album filled with pictures. Of herself and Roselynn and Ellamae. Of Sam and Paul and Dana and of other folks from town.

And of Nate. Lots of pictures of Nate, showing how she'd grown and changed through the years.

He clenched his jaw so hard, the candy split in two. He should've been here for her. He should've been her daddy all along.

A movement through the screened door caught his eye. Tess stood in the entrance hall, looking down at Nate's bent head.

Unaware of her mama's presence, she tugged at the lace on her sneaker. "I guess I'll never have brothers and sisters." Before he could think of what to say, she took a deep breath and added, "Why can't you stay here?"

His turn for a deep breath, one he let out by degrees. "I told you the other day, Nate," he said softly. "I have a ranch to run—in Montana. I'll have to go back there sometime soon. But you'll get to visit. I promised you that, remember?"

"Uh-huh."

She kept fiddling with her sneaker, refusing to meet his

eyes. He could feel Tess's gaze on him now. He kept his focus on Nate.

"So," she continued, "when you go there, are you ever coming here again?"

"Of course I am." But no matter how many times he returned, he would never get back all he'd missed.

He couldn't escape the irony of the situation. Or the parallel between this conversation and those he'd had in past weeks with Tess.

"It's just a quick plane ride," he told Nate. "Montana's not that far away."

"It's far. I looked it up on the computer." She shot to her feet.

He glanced toward the door. Tess no longer stood in the entry.

Nate bolted into the house and yanked the door so roughly, it bounced before slamming shut. The quick slap of her sneakers told him she was running.

"Nate, stop," Tess said from inside the house.

The sound of running steps continued.

As he reached the door, she spoke again. "Anastasia Lynn La—"

"Don't call me that!" Nate shrieked. "My name shoulda been *Cantrell!*"

Her cheeks flushed beet-red, she stood near the stairs and stared back in their direction. Tess had frozen just beside the doorway, her face drained of any color at all.

He stepped into the house, closed the door gently and looked from one to the other of them.

"Nate," he said, "don't be in such a hurry to take on my name. Your own's got a lot more going for it."

She looked down at the toes of her sneakers.

"And," he added, "don't be so quick to sass your mama. She doesn't deserve that kind of talk from you."

There was a lot more Tess didn't deserve.

Roselynn entered the hall from the doorway into the dining room. Her eyes widened when she saw the three of them standing motionless. "What's all this? Tess, did you let Caleb and Nate know supper's waiting? Isn't anyone planning to come eat?"

"I told them," Tess said. "I'm leaving now. Joe just pulled up." She slipped past him and through the doorway without a backward glance. In a hurry to go meet the man. Well, she'd be better off with Harley.

Roselynn turned and went into the dining room again.

Caleb hesitated, then looked toward the stairs.

Nate had disappeared from sight.

He swallowed a taste of guilt more bitter than that lime candy he'd crunched to shards.

Nothing but a burden to me. Nothing but deadweight dragging me down.

His own mama had said that about him, and he hadn't wanted to hear the words. Hadn't wanted to believe them. But he couldn't deny how well they now applied to his relationship with Tess.

Showing up here had done nothing but cause more trouble for her with Nate.

They'd both be better off with him gone.

"Joe," Tess said quietly. She sat in the passenger seat of his car as he drove her home from their date. Early. "I hope you can understand."

"Of course I can, Tess. Come on, now. It's not like I'm just some stranger walking in on this."

"I know. You've always been there for me."

"And your heart's always been with Caleb." He shrugged, his eyes on the road. "Even before you told me tonight, I knew I'd lost my chance."

"I'm sorry."

And she was. Yet her thoughts had already made the leap across town to the Whistlestop.

It had been a crazy week.

Caleb had received what he'd asked for, the chance to get to know Nate better. With her explosion tonight, he might have gotten more than he'd expected.

She would have to talk to Nate in the morning. Not to scold her. How could she scold her daughter, when she felt the same way?

Her name should have been Cantrell, too.

She'd gotten what she'd hoped for, also, the chance to get closer to Caleb. The purchase of the property had given them a lot to discuss, but they'd found other things to talk about, as well.

In silence, Joe turned the corner onto Signal Street.

She couldn't drag her thoughts from Caleb.

Seeing his concern over Nate, watching how much time they'd spent together, she had to believe her hopes would come true. That the temporary agreement she and Caleb had come to for their daughter's sake would lead to a permanent reunion for them.

She and Joe rode the final blocks in silence. When he pulled over to the curb, she could see Caleb in the swing on the front porch. He sat staring out at Signal Street, his expression brooding.

She fumbled for the door handle. "I'll see you at the store, Joe."

"Tess." When she turned to look at him, he reached over and took her hand. "Just so you know, those times I asked you to marry me, that was me talking, nobody else. I asked because I wanted to."

Emotion clogged her throat. She simply nodded and

squeezed his fingers. On the sidewalk, she waited until he'd driven away before turning to walk up the path.

After taking a deep breath and letting it out slowly, she climbed the steps and took the empty half of the swing. Caleb said nothing. After a while, she asked, "How was Nate at suppertime?"

"She didn't show."

She sighed. "I'll speak to her. She needs to apologize. And I owe you an explanation."

"You don't owe me anything."

"Yes, I do. For why I never contacted you later, to tell you about Nate."

He didn't respond.

She licked her suddenly dry lips, then went on, "I told you about my grandfather, how he felt about my going to school. He was strict and hard and unyielding about everything, and I knew if he found out about us, he'd take that away. I made you keep our relationship a secret because I was afraid of that. Afraid of him."

He continued to stare out at the street.

She sagged back against the swing, knowing she faced the most difficult part of her story now. "After Nate came, I didn't try to contact you, either. Granddad wasn't happy about my having a baby, but he knew I was dependent on him." He didn't like that, either, but that wasn't something Caleb ever needed to know. "To give him credit, he took care of me and Nate when she came along. And I was afraid of doing anything to upset that. Anything that would get me into trouble."

He rose from his seat and moved to lean up against the post near the stairs where Nate always sat. "You'd already wound up 'in trouble.'"

The words hung between them for a long moment.

Finally, she nodded, knowing what he meant by the emphasis. "When I first found out I was pregnant, I didn't dare tell anyone. My mother's never been good about keeping things from me...most of the time. She tells Aunt El everything, too. And," she said grimly, "Aunt El's so blunt, she would have told Granddad he drove me to it—and then expect him to accept the news calmly because she was the one who delivered it."

"So you came looking for me."

She nodded again, knowing there was nothing else she could add. He knew the rest.

"I didn't do right by you, Tess. I *am* sorry about that. There's not much I can do about what happened back then. No way we can go back in time."

She held her breath. This was nothing like that throwaway apology he had made the first night they'd seen each other again. The crack in his voice, the shadows in his eyes told her he meant what he'd said. He regretted what happened between them. Maybe even wished, as she did, that they'd always been together.

"I'll do something now," he said.

His determination brought tears to her eyes. Her heart raced, making her pulse flutter. She rose from the swing, began to reach out, but he looked away.

She stood frozen. Then she let her hands fall to her sides.

"Tomorrow," he said, "I'll head back home."

She managed to choke off the cry that rose to her throat. In that one flat statement, he'd shattered all her hopes. Again.

The screened door creaked open, breaking the silence.

Nate stepped out onto the porch. Her eyes were huge and shining and her lips trembled, and Tess longed to reach out to hug her the way she'd wanted to do with Caleb.

But he had already moved across the porch and put his hand on Nate's shoulder.

Nate blinked rapidly and bent her head.

"I'm sorry I was never a part of your life," he said softly, then glanced at Tess. "And I'm sorry I wasn't there for you."

"Me, too," Nate said, staring at her sneakers. "And I'm sorry I listened again. It was just for a minute. I *had* to."

Shaking his head, he looked down at her. He smiled with such tenderness, Tess now could not hold back a small sob.

Nate lifted her jaw to that rebellious angle Tess knew so well. "I heard what you told Mom," she said, her words tumbling together, "and I know you're gonna leave. I want to go, too. I want to live in Montana with you."

Chapter Eighteen

"Go to sleep, now," Tess said.

After she had coaxed Nate upstairs again, it had taken a long while to settle her down enough to get ready for bed.

"But—"

"I told you, honey," she said gently, "we'll all have a lot of talking to do in the morning. And, Nate," she added, forcing more firmness into her tone, "remember what else I told you. Nothing good will come of it if I find you out of your room and anywhere you shouldn't be tonight."

"I know," Nate mumbled, dragging the sheet up almost over her head. "And I said I'm sorry I listened again."

Torn between tears and a smile, Tess leaned down to kiss her forehead. "I'll see you in the morning."

She closed the bedroom door quietly behind her.

As she went down the stairs, she cringed, knowing she hadn't been entirely truthful with Nate. Yes, they would talk in the morning. But by then, the important things would have been said.

She could understand Nate's feelings at the thought that Caleb planned to go off and leave her. How could she not understand, when she'd once suffered through the experience herself? When she'd dreaded it happening once more?

But she'd learned something tonight, with Caleb's announcement. While the thought of losing him again had broken her heart, too, this time she was strong enough to handle it.

The idea of losing her daughter was a whole other subject.

For the second time in her life, Tess was going to take a stand against a man who wanted to force her into a situation she wouldn't accept. And now, it wasn't just her own future at stake, but her daughter's.

Caleb was about to find out just how rebellious *she* could be.

She marched into the living room, where he sat on the couch staring down at a magazine.

She tossed the afghan from the rocker onto the ottoman and took a seat. She didn't need anything to hold on to now—but her temper.

"Caleb, I haven't said this to Nate, but I'm saying it to you. You told her you were sorry you weren't part of her life, and you seemed sincere about it. I'm glad to know that. I'm sorry for the way things worked out for all three of us—though you had a lot to do with that." She paused, pressed her lips together for a long moment, then went on. "I had a lot to do with it, too." Clamping her hands on the rocker's arms, she struggled to keep her voice calm. And failed miserably. "I don't care how much you regret not being around for Nate. You'll never be able to make up for lost time with her. It's gone. Just as you'll be gone, as of tomorrow. But you are *not* taking her with you."

She stared him down, daring him to argue.

He looked back at her for a long time, his green eyes glowing in the light from the table lamp. Finally, he said simply, "Of course not."

She blinked. "Just like that?"

"Yeah, just like that. I don't want Nate with me."

His arrogant tone, so like her grandfather's, stunned her. His careless attitude made her heart hurt. And as irrational as it might be, as a mother she felt overwhelmed by the need to rage at him for the cruelty of his words. How dare he dismiss Nate so coldly?

"You must have one hell of an opinion of me, Tess, if you think I'd take a nine-year-old away from her mama." He laughed just as arrogantly as he'd spoken, and she realized his attitude had been directed at her, not Nate. He rose from the couch. "Good night."

He turned to leave the room. She did nothing to stop him. There was nothing she could do to make the situation any better. Saying anything at all might make things worse.

Nate would stay here with her. That had to be enough.

She had gotten what she'd wanted.

And lost the dream she'd unknowingly been holding on to since the day Caleb had left Flagman's Folly years ago.

CALEB HAD PUT a good number of miles behind him before the sun sent even a glimmer into his rearview mirror. He'd wanted to be away from the inn and out of town long before anyone else was up.

After he'd left Tess in the living room last night, he'd knocked first on Roselynn's door and then on Nate's to say his farewells. Better to do it right away than wait till morning.

Easier than running into Tess again.

Roselynn took the news hard, but he told her she hadn't seen the last of him. He'd be back. He just didn't say when.

Nate stared at him, blinking away tears she wouldn't let fall, and near broke his heart. He tucked her in and kissed her forehead and said goodbye. He told her the same things he'd told Roselynn, but unlike her gram, Nate didn't accept his word. She wouldn't let him leave her room until he'd made promises. So he'd made them, wondering how many he could keep.

Tess...

He didn't want to think about Tess. To think she could even suggest he'd take Nate away from her. It proved how little respect she had for him.

About as much as he had for himself.

He gripped the steering wheel and squinted through the windshield. Now, away from the inn and Flagman's Folly, he could finally get some perspective. And he didn't like what he saw.

The road ahead of him was bare. Empty. At the end of it he would find the airport and the flight home to his ranch in Montana.

Behind him lay the only things that really mattered.

Flagman's Folly itself, the place where he'd found acceptance from folks. Where he'd had it all along, no matter what he'd told himself over the years.

Roselynn and Ellamae, two women who looked out for his interests, something his own mama had never done.

Nate, the daughter who cared about him even though he'd never been a daddy to her.

And Tess.

Again, he didn't want to think about Tess, but he had to face the truth. To admit she had good reason for feeling the way she did about him.

Yet she'd never given him a chance to make peace with her.

With that thought, he acknowledged what he hadn't been able to admit before. What he couldn't put into words even now.

And with that thought, he also knew he couldn't go.

For better or for worse, he had to tell Tess how he felt.

He had to hope she could find it in her heart to let him make up for his past mistakes.

Leaving the bare road ahead, he gunned the engine and swung the truck in a tight, hard U-turn. A loud thump sounded from the back of the truck, and he muttered under his breath. He'd forgotten about his suitcase.

But suitcases didn't yell "Ow!"

He pulled to the side of the road and parked with his flashers going. After he'd walked around to the back of the truck, he rested his crossed arm on the edge of the tailgate and waited.

When he had put the suitcase into the truck bed that morning, he'd seen the tarps he had tossed in there after he'd finished painting and then had forgotten to bring them back to Sam. He'd shrugged, figuring he would have the car rental place get rid of them. Sam wouldn't lose sleep over a couple of drop cloths.

Now a pair of hands crept out from the edge of a tarp and pushed it aside. Nate sat up and stared at him.

"Good morning," he said. "How's everything?"

"Coulda been fine, except that big bag rolled over and squished me."

"Are you hurt?"

"No, I'm okay." She paused, then said tentatively, "Are you mad 'cause I'm here?"

"No. But what brings you here?"

"You did." She sounded surprised. She crawled across the truck bed over to where he still stood with his arms on the tailgate. Slowly, she rose to her knees in front of him and looked him in the eye. "I got in the truck because I didn't know what time you were leaving. Then I fell asleep."

"I told you last night," he reminded her quietly, "I can't take you with me."

"But I thought if I hid till we got to the airport, you'd have to."

"Nate…"

"Never mind." She gave a long, drawn-out sigh. "I can't go, anyway. I can't leave Becky and Gram and Aunt El. And Mom." She squinted and looked away, but not before he saw the tears filling her eyes. "I know I fight with her a lot. I'll try to get better about that. 'Cause I really need my mom." She blinked, swallowed hard and looked back at him. "But I…I need a daddy, too."

His chest tightened until he could barely breathe. He had to blink several times, himself.

He could see in Nate's eyes and face how she felt. She couldn't say the words yet, and he wouldn't, either. It was too soon for both of them.

But she loved him. As much as he loved her.

His daughter loved him. The knowledge gave him confidence even as it raised another question in his mind.

Could her mother ever love him, too?

"You look kinda funny," she said. "You sure you didn't stop the truck 'cause you're mad at me?"

"No, I'm not mad at all. I didn't know you were here."

"Then why?"

"I was headed home."

"That's why you almost killed me with that bag?"

Swallowing a laugh, he nodded.

She looked past him and then over her shoulder, east and west along the highway. Her eyes widened in astonishment. "This truck's going back to Flagman's Folly!"

"So are we, Anastasia Lynn."

"Really? Wow!" She grinned. "Okay…Daddy." She flung her arms around his neck and hugged him tight. "Let's go home."

SHE'D LOOKED everywhere, and still, she couldn't find Nate.

Tess tried to stay calm, to keep from letting her mom know how upset she was. She must have succeeded, because when she went to the kitchen to share the news of Nate's disappearance, Roselynn simply gave a rueful shake of her head.

"Oh, sugar, don't fret. She's probably just run off again to Lissa's like she did the other day."

"I'm not sure about that. I imagine when Caleb told you last night he was leaving, he stopped by Nate's room, too. I think she's run away over that, because when I went up there a couple of hours ago, she was already gone."

That got her mother's attention. *"Before 5:00 a.m.?"*

Nate never woke up that early. Tess didn't often, either, but then, she'd never gone to sleep last night. "Yes," she said, "before five."

"Have you called Dana?"

She nodded. "Nate wasn't there."

"How about the other girls?"

"I didn't want to try them too early. Besides, you know Nate would go to Lissa."

"But it's been two hours. Or more."

"I know. I'm going to call the girls after I check the house one more time, just to make sure she's not hiding somewhere." She had gotten as far as the dining room when she heard the front door open.

She hurried to the doorway and gave a sigh of relief when her daughter entered the house.

"Nate! Where in the world have you—?"

Caleb stepped into the entryway behind Nate and closed the door. He put a hand on Nate's shoulder. "She was with me."

He'd taken Nate with him, after all? Immediately, she shook her head. No, of course, he wouldn't have done that.

As if he'd read her thoughts, he said, "She stowed away in the truck."

Nate nodded emphatically. "Yeah, I hid in the back. He didn't know I was there."

As calmly as she could, Tess nodded. She and Nate would discuss her new habit of running away some other time. Right now, she felt so relieved to see her daughter, she could have cried.

But she hated herself for the briefest second of hope she'd felt when Caleb had stepped into the house. He had come back only to return Nate.

She looked at him and said stiffly, "Thank you for bringing her home."

"He was coming back, too, Mom. He turned the truck around *before* he found me."

Tess nodded again. But she couldn't read anything into that. She knew better than to believe in her dream.

"Nate," Caleb said, "your mama and I have an errand to run. Why don't you go find your gram and tell her we'll be back in an hour or so?"

"Sure."

She smiled up at him, and he ruffled her hair.

Tess had to blink away tears.

Nate crossed the entryway and almost threw her off balance with an unexpected hug. Then she slipped past her into the dining room and shouted, "Hey, Gram, what's for breakfast?"

Her voice faded, her footsteps did, too, and still Caleb stood in the doorway. "Can we talk?" he asked. "Away from here?"

Shrugging, she nodded. Talk couldn't hurt her. Not any more than she hurt already.

Chapter Nineteen

Caleb drove down Signal Street and a good way farther, needing to pull his thoughts together.

Nate had chattered all the back to the Whistlestop, leaving him no time to figure out how to tell Tess what he needed to say. He'd never been much good at talking about things. And he'd never faced any conversation as important as this one.

In the passenger seat, Tess sat with her eyes forward and her fingers twined together in her lap.

When they reached the edge of town, he pulled to the side of the road and cut the ignition. The engine noise died, leaving nothing but silence.

He hoped this conversation wouldn't end the way their talk had finished the night before, with him vowing to leave town. He didn't know what to say to prevent that. He didn't even know where to start, except with some hard truths.

He pushed open the driver's door. "Come on, I've got something I want to show you."

When they had both exited the truck, he led her across the road, past the collection of ramshackle houses and tar-paper shacks to the place he'd once had to call home.

He'd come here again a week ago. Hard as he'd found it to believe, he'd discovered the trailer he had once lived in still sat way in the back, its rusted hulk twenty years more decrepit, its curtains hanging in shreds.

Now he stopped a few feet away from the trailer.

Tess's expression told him she wouldn't need an explanation of why he'd brought her here. Still, he needed to give one.

"This is where I come from," he said, scuffing his boot against the weed-choked ground. He looked from a broken wooden fence to the rusted trailer and then beyond them to a blue sky that went as far as his eye could see. "I couldn't wait for the day I'd leave this behind me. And the day I'd leave this town. I guess we pretty much covered that already."

"Yes," she said, so softly he could barely hear her.

"I hated Flagman's Folly and almost everyone in it. I thought folks looked down on me because I was dirt-poor and had no daddy. But mostly because of the kind of mama I had. All I could think of was getting the hell out. And then I started seeing you." He took a deep breath and let it out slowly. "This next part probably won't make a lot of sense. Back then, I'd never have brought you here, but after we'd gone together a while, I got resentful that you wouldn't take me to your house or introduce me to your family. You wouldn't even let anyone know we were going together."

"Caleb—"

"It's all right," he interrupted, knowing if he didn't get this out he might never have another chance. Or the nerve. "We covered that, too. I understand why now, but back then I didn't know. I thought you looked down on me, too. The only thing I could figure to do was prove myself to you. To everyone."

Tess moved away, and his heart seemed to lurch.

She stopped a few feet from the trailer, where some kids

had piled cinder blocks together to make a small house or a fort. She sat down on one of the walls and looked at him, her expression neutral.

Seeing her settle made his heart settle down again, too.

"Once I got away from here," he continued, "my life changed. For the good. That night you came to Gallup, that night I had my first win, felt like a sign that I'd done the right thing. I'd made a start. But I knew one win wouldn't get me far. When you showed up, I was fixated on getting that trophy so I could show you what I'd done. Only I went about it like a jackass. We covered that, too."

He shoved his hands into his back pockets. The next words didn't want to come, but he had to say them. "Then you told me you were getting married. And I swear to you, Tess, nothing in my life had ever hurt that bad."

He heard her let out a half sigh but couldn't look at her. Not yet.

"I felt like I had nothing left. Nothing but the rodeo. I went on to win all those trophies and buckles you talked about. Won a lot of money, too. I had sponsors lining up to sign me, buckle bunnies hanging on my arms. They proved I was someone. Someone important. Not just Mary Cantrell's bastard son." He clenched his jaw so hard, he thought he might crack a molar or two.

"I told you—" she began.

"I know you did. Wait, please. Or I may never get to finish." He continued more slowly. "After that, I didn't think about Flagman's Folly very often. But when I got thrown from that bull and wound up in the hospital, and then all during the physical therapy at the rehab, I had a lot of thinking time on my hands. And I thought about what they'd told me—I almost didn't make it."

The memory alone made his bad knee twinge. He moved over to the steadiest-looking section of the broken wooden fence and leaned back against it. Then he slid his foot up to plant his boot flat against the post, removing some of the pressure. From his knee, not his confession.

"The doctor's news brought me up short, I tell you. Made me take a look at what I wanted to do with my life. Or what was left of it. I needed to start over again. But I knew I couldn't move forward, until I could finally shake off my past. Until I'd come back here and done what I'd sworn I'd do, show everybody I was just as good as they were." He laughed shortly. "Only, nobody appeared to think I *wasn't* just as good. They all seemed to like me fine. Dori and Manny at the Double S. Judge Baylor and your aunt, Ellamae. Sam and Ben.

"That day at Ben's, when you and Ellamae left, Judge Baylor told me I'd always had a chip on my shoulder. The more I talked to folks and saw how they acted with me, the more I realized the judge was right. But getting to know folks knocked that chip right off."

Now he could look at her again. Even from here, he could see her eyes shining with tears. The sight almost broke him, but he couldn't go to her until he had earned the right.

"I learned something else, too. It didn't matter if I was poor or not then. It doesn't matter that I'm rich now. Folks aren't measuring my worth by my bank account but by the respect I show them. And the respect I have for myself."

He hadn't had the courage to open his heart completely to Tess until now. Watching her, he saw the dark curls he'd never been able to keep from threading his fingers through, the dark eyes he'd always loved to gaze into. Those eyes held so much more now, and so did Tess herself. An inner fire and an inner strength—both equal to the ones he'd have to draw upon now.

He braced himself, knowing he'd have to lay himself

bare, tell her things he hadn't understood himself. Until today.

"Respect for myself was something I *didn't* have, till I turned that truck around this morning to come back to town today. Because I knew I wouldn't leave again without telling you the truth. About everything." He shook his head. "I'd made my peace with everyone but you. And I figured out why. I need more than just peace from you, Tess, because you mean the most to me."

Now he had to look her straight in those dark eyes when he said what came next. She sat staring at him, her lips pressed together, her hands flat against the cinder block wall.

"I ran off ten years ago, after convincing myself everyone looked down on me. I ran out on you, and you were the best thing I had in my life." His hands trembled. He rested them on the fence rail to steady himself. "I ran out on you again today. This time, I didn't want to leave, I swear. But I thought I had to give up what I wanted—to do the right thing for you and Nate. Now I know that's not true. I should've listened to my instincts. And now I want to come back. If you'll have me."

Accepting he still couldn't go to her, knowing he wasn't done, he held on to the railing for all he was worth. Which wasn't much. And never would be, if she wouldn't take him on again.

Trying to keep herself from going to Caleb, Tess grasped the cinder blocks so tightly the rough concrete dug into her palms.

She'd seen the struggle reflected in his face, in his stance, and the depth of emotion in his eyes. She'd heard all he had said till now. Words she had always longed to hear. But did she really understand them? "You mean... you want your room back again?"

"That'll do for starters, if it's the way it has to be." He gave a half smile that made her heart beat faster. "But to be honest, I'm hoping that option won't last long at all. Because I want a permanent reservation. A place here with you. Being a husband and daddy. Everything all rolled up into one."

She opened her mouth, but before she could speak, he shook his head and moved to take a seat on the wall beside her. He studied her, his eyes clear but his expression troubled.

"Please hear me out," he continued. "I know I can't expect you to take me up on just my say-so that I'm ready now, when I wasn't before. Or that I've changed." He shook his head ruefully. "To tell you the truth, just a few weeks ago, I'd never have expected to be saying all this. And there's more."

He lifted her hand from the wall between them, rubbed his thumb across her knuckles, the way he'd always done years ago. His hand was calloused now. His touch was familiar, yet changed. So were they.

"Once I got back here, at some point, I finally realized I'd come for your forgiveness. But the longer I stayed, the more I realized I hadn't earned it yet. And then I realized even more. Hard to admit," he said slowly, "but I don't think I knew the reason that mattered most until this morning when I found myself leaving you again. I love you."

His eyes brightened with the light of sincerity and hope…and something else. Her throat closed so tightly, she could barely breathe.

"I can't change what happened, Tess, and I know we've lost so much since then. But I want to make up for it. If I can."

He squinted, and the skin around his eyes crinkled.

Though she couldn't see the tears in his eyes, she heard that emotion in his voice. "You're the only woman I've ever loved. The only person who gave me love unconditionally. What's more, you're real with me."

He squeezed her fingers gently, as if to prove his point, and she felt her chest tighten, too.

"Those buckle bunnies you keep talking about—all those women hanging on me for all those years. They didn't want me. They worshipped my fame and fortune, that's it. I don't want that. I want your reality. I want *you.* Now. And forever."

He released her hand and sat back, waiting.

Still, she couldn't catch her breath. Rising, she moved to lean against the fence where he'd stood previously, needing the distance from him. The perspective. Needing the railing to keep her from falling.

Not falling for Caleb's words. She didn't have any doubt of the truth of them.

Not falling down in a heap on the dusty ground. She felt stronger than she ever had in her life.

But to keep from falling into his arms.

Bowing her head, she held on to the railing, one hand on either side of her as Caleb had done.

She knew he'd said what he had to and was waiting for her to begin. So she did.

"When you left us this morning, I knew I'd be strong enough to survive it. I've grown that much since you left the first time." She gave a half laugh that sounded more like a sob. "Back then, I wasn't so sure I'd make it. When you left me, I hated you. I never wanted to see you again."

He shifted, yet made no move to come to her. She felt grateful for that.

"Then I discovered I was pregnant. When Granddad found out, eventually, he tried to force me into a marriage.

I told the boy I couldn't marry him. And I've told him that every time he's asked me since."

"Harley." He spoke softly and shook his head in wonder.

She nodded.

"Good old Joe," he said with a crooked smile. "I owe that man."

She would have smiled back, if she hadn't had to brace herself for what came next. "Once Granddad put his foot down, I had nowhere else to go. Except to you." Her voice shook so badly, she needed to wait a moment before she could continue. "When you were there in that arena, with your buckle bunnies and your trophy and the announcer calling your name, something inside me snapped."

"Tess—"

Though she heard the pain in his voice, she shook her head. "No, Caleb. Not till you've heard me out. I let my pride get the best of *me* then. You didn't give me a chance to tell you about the baby. But I didn't take a stand and tell you, anyway. Instead, I came home and stood up to my grandfather, who only wanted me to get married to give the baby a name." She swallowed hard and looked at him, knowing he would see the tears in her eyes. Hoping he could see her sincerity now, too.

"That's why I told you—and how I can feel so sure it's true—that not knowing your own daddy's name doesn't matter. Nate never knew hers. That doesn't make her any less a person. Or make me love her less. I wasn't going to get married just to keep Granddad happy. Or to give our baby a name that wasn't yours."

A tear spilled down her cheek, but she couldn't reach up to brush it away. Her hands were still clamped on the fence rail. Now it *had* become the only thing holding her up.

This time, when Caleb shifted, it was to rise and cross the space between them. She felt grateful for that, too.

He thumbed away the tear that had trickled down to the corner of her mouth. His hand lingered there, brushing her jaw, tilting her chin up.

"I'm sorry," she said. "I was wrong not to tell you about the baby."

"I was wrong in a lot of ways, too. I love you, Tess. I just hope you can love me again."

"That's something else I've learned since you've come home." She smiled tentatively, trying to hold back her tears. "Even when I thought I hated you, I never stopped loving you."

He wrapped his arms around her and pulled her close, nestled her head beneath his chin. She could feel the pulse in his neck pounding and his heart thundering against hers.

They stood that way for a long time, and their heartbeats gradually returned to a steady pace. She knew she'd never been happier.

But then Caleb kissed her and said the one thing that could make her happier still. The one thing she'd hoped all these years to hear.

"Let's get married, Tess."

ONCE CALEB HAD turned away to leave the rusted shell of the trailer behind, he knew he would never go back there again. He'd never want the reminder of a life no kid should live. Never need to see the place that had made him believe he deserved less than anyone else.

When he and Tess reached the Whistlestop Inn and crossed the yard to the back porch, he had to pause for a moment to hold her close again. To take in all that he *did* deserve.

Self-respect. A home and family. Tess.

He heard the back door open.

They both turned to look.

Nate stood on the porch with her hand still on the door latch, as if unsure whether or not she should stay. "I wasn't listening," she assured them.

"We weren't saying anything," he returned.

"Yeah, I noticed. You look funny, Mom."

"I feel funny. The happy kind." Smiling, Tess squeezed his hand. "Your daddy just asked me to marry him."

Nate's eyes widened. "Really? Wow! I gotta tell Gram and Aunt El!" She bounded through the door, then stopped and turned back. "I'm coming to the wedding," she added, "but don't expect me to wear a dress."

The door slammed against the frame. They could hear her shrieking as she ran through the kitchen.

Tess laughed. "I don't know," she said, drawing the words out and shaking her head. "Are you sure you understand what you're asking? If you want reality, you'll get it here. A meddling mother-in-law and an aunt who's worse. A belligerent preteen daughter. And a wife who gets rebellious at times, too."

"Yes, I'm sure."

A flash of movement against a windowpane caught his eye. Nate and Roselynn and Ellamae had all gathered at the dining room window and stood smiling down at him.

He smiled back, then looked at Tess again. "Don't worry about me," he said. "After riding my share of angry bulls, I can handle a few ornery women."

* * * * *

HEART & HOME

Heartwarming romances where love can
happen right when you least expect it.

COMING NEXT MONTH
AVAILABLE MARCH 13, 2012

#1393 COWBOY SAM'S QUADRUPLETS
Callahan Cowboys
Tina Leonard

#1394 THE RELUCTANT TEXAS RANCHER
Legends of Laramie County
Cathy Gillen Thacker

#1395 COLORADO FIREMAN
Creature Comforts
C.C. Coburn

#1396 COWBOY TO THE RESCUE
The Teagues of Texas
Trish Milburn

REQUEST YOUR FREE BOOKS!
2 FREE NOVELS PLUS 2 FREE GIFTS!

❖ Harlequin®

American ★ Romance®

LOVE, HOME & HAPPINESS

YES! Please send me 2 FREE Harlequin® American Romance® novels and my 2 FREE gifts (gifts are worth about $10). After receiving them, if I don't wish to receive any more books, I can return the shipping statement marked "cancel." If I don't cancel, I will receive 4 brand-new novels every month and be billed just $4.49 per book in the U.S. or $5.24 per book in Canada. That's a saving of at least 14% off the cover price! It's quite a bargain! Shipping and handling is just 50¢ per book in the U.S. and 75¢ per book in Canada.* I understand that accepting the 2 free books and gifts places me under no obligation to buy anything. I can always return a shipment and cancel at any time. Even if I never buy another book, the two free books and gifts are mine to keep forever.

154/354 HDN FEP2

Name	(PLEASE PRINT)

Address	Apt. #

City	State/Prov.	Zip/Postal Code

Signature (if under 18, a parent or guardian must sign)

Mail to the **Reader Service:**
IN U.S.A.: P.O. Box 1867, Buffalo, NY 14240-1867
IN CANADA: P.O. Box 609, Fort Erie, Ontario L2A 5X3

Not valid for current subscribers to Harlequin American Romance books.

Want to try two free books from another line?
Call 1-800-873-8635 or visit www.ReaderService.com.

* Terms and prices subject to change without notice. Prices do not include applicable taxes. Sales tax applicable in N.Y. Canadian residents will be charged applicable taxes. Offer not valid in Quebec. This offer is limited to one order per household. All orders subject to credit approval. Credit or debit balances in a customer's account(s) may be offset by any other outstanding balance owed by or to the customer. Please allow 4 to 6 weeks for delivery. Offer available while quantities last.

Your Privacy—The Reader Service is committed to protecting your privacy. Our Privacy Policy is available online at www.ReaderService.com or upon request from the Reader Service.

We make a portion of our mailing list available to reputable third parties that offer products we believe may interest you. If you prefer that we not exchange your name with third parties, or if you wish to clarify or modify your communication preferences, please visit us at www.ReaderService.com/consumerchoice or write to us at Reader Service Preference Service, P.O. Box 9062, Buffalo, NY 14269. Include your complete name and address.

HAR11B

Get swept away with author

CATHY GILLEN THACKER

and her new miniseries

Legends of Laramie County

On the Cartwright ranch, it's the women
who endure and run the ranch—and it's time for
lawyer Liz Cartwright to take over. Needing some help
around the ranch, Liz hires Travis Anderson, a fellow
attorney, and Liz's high-school boyfriend. Travis says
he wants to get back to his ranch roots, but Liz knows
Travis is running from something. Old feelings emerge
as they work together, but Liz can't help but wonder
if Travis is home to stay.

Reluctant Texas Rancher

**Available March
wherever books are sold.**

www.Harlequin.com

There came a time in a man's life when he knew he was well and truly caught. Devon Carter stared down at the diamond ring nestled in velvet and acknowledged that this was one such time. He snapped the lid closed and shoved the box into the breast pocket of his suit.

He had two choices. He could marry Ashley Copeland and fulfill his goal of merging his company with Copeland Hotels, thus creating the largest, most exclusive line of resorts in the world, or he could refuse and lose it all.

Put in that light, there wasn't much he could do except pop the question.

The doorman to his Manhattan high-rise apartment hurried to open the door as Devon strode toward the street. He took a deep breath before ducking into his car, and the driver pulled into traffic.

Tonight was the night. All of his careful wooing, the countless dinners, kisses that started brief and casual and became more breathless—all a lead-up to tonight. Tonight his seduction of Ashley Copeland would be complete, and then he'd ask her to marry him.

He shook his head as the absurdity of the situation hit him for the hundredth time. Personally, he thought William Copeland was crazy for forcing his daughter down Devon's throat.

Ashley was a sweet enough girl, but Devon had no desire

to marry anyone.

William had other plans. He'd told Devon that Ashley had no head for the family business. She was too softhearted, too naive. So he'd made Ashley part of the deal. The catch? Ashley wasn't to know of it. Which meant Devon was stuck playing stupid games.

Ashley was supposed to think this was a grand love match. She was a starry-eyed woman who preferred her animal-rescue foundation over board meetings, charts and financials for Copeland Hotels.

If she ever found out the truth, she wouldn't take it well.

And hell, he couldn't blame her.

But no matter the reason for his proposal, before the night was over, she'd have no doubts that she belonged to him.

What will happen when Devon marries Ashley?
Find out in Maya Banks's passionate new novel
TEMPTED BY HER INNOCENT KISS
Available March 2012 from Harlequin Desire!